The Dreams of Mattie Fitch

B.D. Mashack

The Dreams of Mattie Fitch
by B.D. Mashack

All Rights Reserved
©2014 B.D. Mashack

FIRST EDITION
ISBN: 978-0-9895554-5-6

Published by Happy Publishing
Book Design by Laura Fisher

Printed in the United States of America

Dedication

I lovingly dedicate this book to my mom, Billye Pauline Pittman (b. 4/1935 – 10/30/2011) who inspired and loved me and is now smiling down from Heaven, my children Erica, Erin, Lyle and granddaughter Skye, who just loved me through the hard times and now will celebrate the blessings!. To my four sisters (Lazetta, Pamela, Kristina, Kristal), two brothers (Michael, Jay) for your words of encouragement, and support I love you. And a host of nieces and nephews, family and friends too many to mention who have prayed, cried and gave me support through this blessing, THANK YOU!

Thank you to my Hayward USD family/friends at Anthony W. Ochoa Middle School for your love and support, and Lee Thomas for lighting that fire under my feet with your words.

Lastly, to Jesus Christ whom without whom none of this would be possible!

Introduction

Mattie Fitch was birthed in me thru a close call with an illness in 2005. In my recovery Mattie Fitch entered my dreams and would not allow me the rest until I began to speak about the need to bring her to life on not only the pages of a book, but to the television and big screen.

Writing "The Dreams of Mattie Fitch" has been one of the greatest joys of my life, and has given me hope for all things to come. The connection that Mattie and I have can't be broken, we share a special bond through our belief that all things are possible to them that believe. I look forward to allowing this book and the ones to come to heal the lives of all who read it and bring hope to the hopeless, life to the lifeless and open the eyes of those that have decided to live closed off from the opportunities to dream. Mattie and I believe that "your dreams are your reality asleep, wake them up!" and live again.

CONTENTS

Chapter One
The Dreamer

One year before the Great Depression of 1929, an aura of timelessness descended on the mysterious town of Darlington, South Carolina. September days were often warm with brisk steady winds, and the nights were often stormy and unforgiving. The gusting wind hurled red dust across the dirt road past the vast array of wooden and shotgun homes, past farms with worn-out roofs with patches of tar and tin that served as reminders of battles lost with Mother Nature. Today's storm would be no different.

Two dry and bumpy main roads intersected right in the middle of town where the courthouse and water well met, just adjacent to the main store. Old townsmen, shuffling slowly and chewing snuff would gather on the front porch of Mashack's Grocery Emporium to reminisce about days gone by and share with visitor's stories about the infamous town well, the giant oak tree and the history of the courthouse.

Just up the road, separated by the towns railroad track, was one part of town where beautiful plantation mansions, many adorned with wrap-around porches, sat proudly among massive trees and tall grass while the porches appeared to smile mysteriously at passersby. These homes were much grander and statelier. Their landscape was meticulous and beautifully colored with fruit trees, flowers and cotton or tobacco fields. Then there was the Negro part of town just over on the other side of the tracks, and after many years everyone knew there was an unspoken rule to "stay on your side of the tracks. The residents worked well with what what they had, and at times the beauty of their shotgun homes was overshadowed by old, unused, boarded-up slave quarters that possessed unwelcome memories of previous days.

No matter what they decided collectively that each family would work together with the others and make life peaceful for all, despite the reality of hatred and racism.

As the day marched on and signs of evening approached, the residents prepared for yet another rainy night. Many of the elders stood on their porches staring off towards the collection of dark billowing clouds. There was eeriness in the air as the wind gathered strength.

"Lookin' like the storm's brewin'" shouted Mr. Brown his cheek slightly protruding from his normal bit of snuff.

"Yes indeed, better get them critters in, it's gonna be a long night," Jake answered, pulling at the straps of his dirty overalls. "I gotta run ta town, but I reckon it kin wait."

The wind began to pick up strength, blowing leaves and dust so fiercely communication was minimal.

It's lookin' like that last storm that killed old man Woods wife and son a few years back so you best be careful, Brown responded, spitting into the red dirt.

In the distance, the sound of church bells ringing non-stop sent confirmation that time was short; the storm was coming. Children, reluctant to give up a few moments of play, began to scatter after hearing their mothers yelling for them from adjacent fields.

Just up the road outside the Fitch's home stood Mattie Fitch.

Her arms wide open, Mattie began spinning slowly round and around, as the wind whirled about her rhythmically as if engaged in a dance. Pausing for a moment she stared off in the distance, blowing leaves gently stroking her cheeks. Sounds of thunder, church bells ringing and the sweet aroma of rain caught her attention. There was something magical about the rain that Mattie adored; it made her dreams more vivid and journeys more real. The dreams Mattie had were more real than anyone knew.

Mattie was the youngest of four children, the only girl. She was best known for her striking brown eyes, and thick ponytails which were often pinned crossways. Her skin, a beautiful bronze, was the result of many hours spent picking tobacco in the hot Carolina sun and lying in her patch of sunflowers that her father Dozier had cleared for her between a patch of sunflowers and tall grass.

Time was short and her mother would soon be calling so she sprinted down to her personal playground off-limits to all. As Mattie approached, the blowing strands of sunflowers and grass seemed to open and embrace her. She stepped into the welcoming abyss which closed mysteriously behind her. Sauntering over to her stack of old quilts she picked up one, unfolded it quickly; she lay down, closed her eyes and instantly began to dream.

Do you hear them? I can't believe all that applause is for me. Oh my god I can't believe it, Robert, can you hear that? I have waited so long: What do you think I should do?

I think that I love you, and I am very proud of you. And you are the most beautiful woman I have ever seen dance. Now stop messing around and get back out there and take another bow!"

As the audience yelled "Bravo," and screamed for an encore, she walked out slowly, bowed gracefully, and walked forward to receive several bouquets of flowers from the patrons who had come to see her perform. She was finally a star. She had danced her way to Broadway, and all of those people had come to see her. It became overwhelming, her heart began pounding as she tried unsuccessfully to catch her breath, fear and panic set in; the lights flashing from all the cameras, patrons screaming her name became too much. Stepping backwards she lost her footing, and started to fall..." oh my God catch her!!"

"Mattie Fitch! Mattie Fitch! You in there?" yelled Leona. "Lord this here chil' is gon' catch herself a chill." She peeked into the tall grass. "Come on yonder, Mattie!"

Leona was a loving and kind, but firm woman, who held her family together like the stitches in her homemade quilts. All day she hummed hymns while she saw to her daily chores. A sense of sadness rested itself in the lines of her face that connected one pain to another. Her beautiful plain face was dark from the years of hard work in the fields, and concern about her family's future.

"Here I am mama, I'm right here!" shouted Mattie, jumping up. "I was just layin' here dreamin', and I was dancin' Mama and the people."

"Girl, slow down...don't you smell that rain a comin'? Get on inside before you catch yourself a chill." Leona, holding her arm tightly scooted her toward the house "you always dreamin' child."

"One of these days, Mama, you'll see, I'm gon' be a dancer, and a doctor, and a teacher, lots of things." Mattie grinned cheerfully excitement filling the air "I have so much to do."

"You gon' be all that, Mattie? I guess you musta forgot that there be certain things that colored folks don't git to do…. but you go 'head and keep right on dreamin', Miss Mattie Fitch, cuz all things are possible.

"I reckon they are cuz that's what you and pa say is in the good Word, and that's that." Mattie smiled innocently, taking a tight hold of Leona's hand.

"I will be watchin' and waitin' cuz dreams ain't nothin' but your reality that's still sleepin'. So you wake it on up, Miss Mattie Fitch."

She paused, smiling solemly at Mattie as their eyes locked in a gaze of hopeful futures.

"Get a move on Mattie that rains a comin'."

In one fell swoop Leona, with Mattie on her heels turned quickly towards the house. They could see the men of the family rushing around trying to make last minute repairs to the roof of the barn, while the others gathered the animals.

"I sure do wish ol man Woods was here to give us a hand I sho' miss my friend," Dozier's hand settled on his chest over his heart. For just a moment he remembered back to the horror of the Woods family drowning.

"I reckon he's not feelin' too good right now. These kinda storms make for a right tough evening I bet, huh Pa?" Michael shuttered.

Dozier nodded. "Yep, but ain't nothin' we kin do bout that right now! He shouted down from the rooftop. "Leona yall get on in the house now!"

If Mattie had her way, they would never patch the holes.

"It's gone be a good one, Ma," looking peacefully up at Leona.

"I think you're right." Leona stroked her hair and kissed the top of her head.

"Come on child! We need to get on inside. I am not in the mood to getting wet, Mattie Fitch," said Leona sternly, as the rain began to fall.

"Aw, Mama I'm comin!"

Mattie skipped onto the porch and yelled up toward Dozier who was making his way off the roof.

"Pa, can I sit on the porch for a bit once suppers done, please?" she pleaded, with excitement and anticipation in her eyes.

Dozier lifted his eyebrows and shrugged his shoulders. "I reckon it might be all right once you finished with your chores,"

"Hey Pa you reckon Mr. Woods is gone be all right tonight?"

"I hope so Mattie, it's been a long time since he's come and worked, but as usual we'll lift him up."

"I dreamed about him a few times, and one of these days I gonna tell him just what I seen because I think it'll make him real happy."

"I sho' miss his corn pie," Leona said sadly.

"I miss my friend," Dozier sighed loudly scratching his head.

Dozier stood motionless, staring toward the road where Woods use to yell that he was on his way. He exhaled, turned and entered the house. No one else spoke.

Mattie quickly finished her chores and eagerly headed out onto the front porch, her smile as bright as the day was dark.

"It's raining even harder now!" she yelled happily through the screen, as she bounced up and down on a loose board.

"Stop that bouncin' Mattie, befo' you fall right through," chided Leona "and put yo' coat on befo' you catch yourself a chill."

The squeaking screen door opened quickly as Leona stepped through carrying Mattie's' dingy brown overcoat.

"Put this on."

"Thank you Mama!" Mattie exclaimed, shoving her arms quickly into the sleeves of the coat, and wrapping them tightly around Leona's waist.

"Thank you fo' what Mattie?"

"For being my Mama I love you."

"I love you too chil, and don't you stay out on dis' here porch too long it's blowin' mighty hard, ya hear?"

"Yes ma'am, I won't. Mama kin I tell you sumthin'?"

"Sho, what is it?"

"Do you know that sometimes I have dreams that give me a fright cuz they always end up happenin'. I remember when Miss Woods and Robert drowned, I saw it in my dreams bout a week befo, but I didn't say nothin'."

"You wuz only bout 6 or 7 Mattie."

"I know, but I seen em drowns Mama. I see lots of thangs, some good, some bad. Do you think somethin's wrong with me?"

"Ain't nothin' wrong wit you Mattie Fitch, you gots what the ole folks calls a gift just be good wit that gift and use it to help, ya hear, don't ever take it ta heart, you just a blessed and special child…..the Lord gonna use you one day that's fo' sho'."

"We betta get on in da house chil, that there wind is whippin' somethin' fierce."

"Yes it is, I reckon you right."

They turned and walked in the house as the wind pressed through the tattered screen slamming it against the frame.

The Lemonade

Pauline appeared quickly, carrying her tray of lemonade and cookies. She was a very pretty woman, tall and slender with a body like a dancer. Her smile gave way to a slight gap which caused her to often cover her mouth with embarrassment when she smiled.

"Come on girls," Pauline said. "The lemonade is here."

Pamela and Mattie skipped over and sat down on the steps of the Miles' front porch which wrapped around their beautiful plantation home like the arms of a loving grandmother. Beautifully colored flowers were arranged perfectly alongside the long black driveway which stretched away from the house toward the main road.

"Here we are girls," said Pauline. "Be careful, no spills ladies."

"Oh, thank you mother!!!" Pamela exclaimed, taking a glass and passing one to Mattie.

"Oh Miss Pauline, thank you ma'am" echoed Mattie. "Yo lemonade is so good!

"Mother, could you hand us our reading book? I want to study some more with Mattie while we drink our lemonade."

"Of course."

The girls loved to drink lemonade, eat the cookies and teach Mattie to read after practicing holding her breath in the water barrel.

Pauline returned with a brown leather book that Pamela had put together especially for Mattie.

As they sat sipping lemonade staring aimlessly down the driveway, Pamela glanced innocently at Mattie.

"I'll always be here for you Mat," softly, "I hope you know that?"

"Sho' I do Pamela, you my best-friend in dis' whole wide world," Mattie replied, surprised, sliding over from her spot and right next to Pamela.

"And no matter what happens, we gon' be together. I just wanted you to know that I won't break my promise, Mattie," Pamela says seriously.

"I knows you won't Pamela," her beautiful brown eyes twinkling innocently. "So let's seal it with our pinkies!" said Mattie abruptly.

"Our pinkies Mattie?" She laughed.

"Yes indeed put yo' pinkie up just like dis here!" Their fingers interlocked in a bond of racial beauty, one black, one white.

Mashack's Emporium

Mattie strolled down the dusty red dirt road towards the store, kicking little rocks that were scattered about and humming her favorite hymn. When she wasn't playing with Pamela she was often found talking with a few of the town elders who were always watching for her from a distance.

"Hey, here she comes!" smiled one elder as he sucked the stick of straw between his teeth.

"That chil' has a gift I tells ya, I ain't neva seen nobody who kin tells you 'bout somethin' that's happenin' and somethin' that's gone happen all in da same breath," he said, looking intently at the others.

"I hears ya, that thar chil's been here befo, that's fo' sho, I still can't believe she is just 12-year-old child?" spoke another elder.

"All I knows is she kin tell me anythang, anytime."

"Afternoon elders, how's everybody?" Mattie said excitedly.

Her big brown eyes and inviting smile embraced everyone standing around.

"Hey Miss Mattie, how you doin'? " The men replied in unison.

"Hey Mattie, what'd ya dream bout' lately? Ya got any-thin to tells us'?" asked a regular.

He reached down into an old freezer, pulling out a soda pop. She was often treated to a cool drink for sharing her dreams with them.

"Tell us a good one now hear, Miss Mattie Fitch. We gots a cool drank just fo' ya," coaxed another elder.

Mattie was always excited to share her dreams with anyone who needed to be lifted up and always knew what they needed to hear.

"I dreamt I was flying this time. I could see a house in the background and there was a man cryin' cuz he dun' lost his wife and son in a storm. He had him a bottle of moonshine he drank day and night cause he thought it wuz gon' make him feel better, but it only made it worse. He blamed himself cuz he told them to wait on the wrong side of the water and his life was never the same again. He became the meanest man in town. Everyone was afraid of him cuz no one understood him, so they made up scary stories bout him. They just didn't know that his heart was broke."

This day Old Man Woods stood in the background dressed in his standard dusty blue coveralls that were terribly worn at the knees. His head full of uncombed graying hair was hidden by a beat-up cowboy hat always pulled down so far no one could see his forlorn eyes. Unable to move as he listened to Mattie's dream caused the hairs on the back of his neck to stand at attention. Frozen, he listened.

"In my dream I seen him sittin' at home wishin' he had one last dance with her. They loved to do that. He was rememberin' how they put their son between em on his feet and would dance, he was singing, laughing and staring happily. Then suddenly the man wrapped his arms around in the air as if he was holding her, then he closed his eyes and mouthed "I love you." He took a few steps back and began to dance around the room all by himself.

Tears filled Old Man Woods eyes. He was mesmerized.

"Then he just stopped, laid his head back an' looked up towards the sky and said out loud "thank you." 'cause I think they had danced again and his wife and son is right proud of him, they don't want him to be sad no more and he gotta go on and trust again 'cause one day things gon' be right. I reckon it's all right fo' a man to cry and folks ought not be pointin' fingers and whisperin', 'cause all he needs is a friend."

There was complete silence. Others stood dumbfounded.

"You reckon that man will ever be happy agin, Miss Mattie?" asked Mr. Woods somberly, stepping down off the porch.

"I reckon so, Mr. Woods", said Mattie intently. "But it's up ta him to decide if'n he wanna be happy or not."

She walked confidently over to where he was standing.

"I reckon that if'n he wants to be happy then he'll need to start doin' thangs that makes him happy."

She grabbed his hand and smiled lovingly. Woods looked down into her innocent

child eyes and smiled for the first time in years.

"Has nobody neva told you that you's an angel, Miss Mattie Fitch," Mr. Woods said emotionally.

"I don't right members anyone sayin' that exactly Mr. Woods, but my folks always says that you gotta be da best, and the rest just happens." Squeezing his hand tightly. There was a quiet silence as she stared up into his weary face, "but nobody right knows but him," she replied.

There was a moment of peaceful stillness then a few peculiar looks.

Mr. Woods took a seat on the porch step, pushed up his shirtsleeves, and just stared off blankly, stroking his chin and twisting the hair in his tangled beard.

Mattie walked over, grabbed her soda and sat down next to Woods. "We miss ya round by the house, and I know Pa misses his friend, and we all miss those corn pies."

They both chuckled.

"I got to get on home now, but I reckon we'll see ya right soon," Mattie smiled winking.

"I reckon that might be so Miss Mattie Fitch."She stood up quickly and headed off down the road, as the group watched with admiration. Turning one last time she waved her hand in the air, "I'll see ya next time," she yelled, skipping down the road.

Finally, Mr. Woods stood, dusted himself, and smiled genuinely looking around at the group. He tipped his hat and walked quietly down the road.

There was nothing else to be done. Mattie had touched another.

"That chil is somethin else. I members when she tol me dat one of my youngins wuz gon choke on a plum an she wuz right an saved his life and my family a whole lot of sadness." Spoke one of the elders.

"Oh yes sa", how bouts when she told the Buford's bout dat fire she seent in they barn."

"You sho is right, and it catched a fire an dey knew'd just what to do," another interrupted.

"She saved me from bein' strung up by mista bout 5 years ago, an I owes dat chil my life an I can't never be able to gives her da thanks she needs to have, but I'll does anythang I kin to help her and they family dats fo sho."

"I'z rememba when she told da mayor bout somethin' and I hear he goes and speaks wit her at dey house," one elder laughing loudly.

"Huh, ain't dat sumthin'? White folks go an sees a little black chil', I wish I was sittin' on dat wall and heard what he had to say."

"All I gots to say is if'n she ever sees anythang bout me, I wants to know cuz God speaks through that chil an she is blessin' folks lives and some don't even know it." One spoke seriously.

"Yes indeed, she is one special chil."

There was suddenly a peaceful quiet and the conversation ended. The men separated giving slight tips of the hat and a polite smile.

Chapter 2
Let's Swing

It was a hot summer afternoon and Mattie and Pamela, who had been playing in the yard, saw some of the kids heading down the road towards the giant oak tree. The tree, which the children had nicknamed "The Giant," had become the gathering and cooling place.

The roots of the tree were massive, reaching up out of the ground and gripping the soil like claws of a grizzly bear. The tree's strong mighty branches and limbs extended outward toward the sky like muscular arms.

The Giant had not always provided a safe refuge. And often times the kids would sit around and laugh about different incidents that had occurred over the years.

"Momma," yelled Pamela, "me and Mattie gon' run over to the Giant for a bit."

"All right, y'all be careful ya hear." Pauline beckoned from inside.

The girls headed quickly down the driveway and arrived quickly and noticed the group huddled under the tree.

"What y'all doin?" asked Mattie breathlessly.

"Aw nuthin', just tryin to stay cool," spoke one of the kids.

"Yeah we was talkin' 'bout ol' times and thangs that happened here at the Giant," interjected another.

"Oh y'all remember what happened to Wayne?"

This memory instantly 'caused a roar of laughter among all the kids sitting around, everyone except Wayne.

"No, I ain't never heard bout that befo'," yelled out a new kid.

"Okay, I'll tell ya," interjected one of the boys.

"Wayne over here," pointing at him and trying not to laugh, "almost drowned after we dared him to swing on the Giant. I reckon he was tired of us teasin' him."

Mumbling and chuckling broke out among the group.

"Right, so we told him that if'n he swang we'd let 'em in," interrupted another, "so he said 'yeah' and we headed on down to the creek. I tell ya it musta spread like a fire 'cause kids from all over Darlington County showed up."

"Wayne was sweatin' real badly. I reckon he was nervous, but he had that look in his eyes," echoed another, laughing.

"Oh yeah and then Roland and Tess showed up," interrupted Pamela.

"What y'all 'bout to do?" slurred Ron.

"Wayne's 'bout to swang!" yelled the children.

Tess snatched the rope and looked over at Wayne, who was trying to look afraid.

"Come on and get on dis' here rope scardy cat!"

"I ain't scared, don't cha see me comin'!" Wayne spoke back.

Walking slowly, Wayne began to unbutton his shirt but quickly closed it at the sounds of snickering from the crowd. He looked back and forth anxiously for a friendly face, and exhaled deeply after finding Mattie and Pamela, who were standing with his little sister Patricia-Ann. They smiled in support.

All at once he headed straight for the rope, building momentum.

"Give it here, I got it," he responded confidently.

"You can do it, don't be afraid," yelled the girls as he passed by.

He nodded his head in agreement, while beads of sweat were rising and falling down his face.

Wayne gained momentum as he reached the tree. Snatching the rope from Tess who was laughing uncontrollably, he stepped on the ledge that they had rigged for swinging. He looked down, then up towards the sky……….. and jumped!

"Lord, get out the way!" yelled one of the boys.

Wayne had not let go on the first swing out and headed back toward the crowd at full speed. The children scrambled as gasps and roars of laughter filled the air and the crowd yelled enthusiastically!

"Let go!" hollered the kids, and that's just what he did.

Wayne hit the water so hard that those standing near the edge received a watery surprise, as roars of laughter erupted.

"I can't swim. Help me!" He screamed.

Panic engulfed the crowd. The girls ran towards the edge yelling frantically, "Wayne! Turn over!"

He was panic-stricken.

All at once, the Duncan clan pressed through the crowd, making a chain between them. Marvin, the eldest, grabbed a stick and headed into the water. After several unsuccessful attempts he grabbed Wayne by the collar with the stick allowing enough time for Wayne to grasp a hold. The terror on Wayne's face was evident, but Marvin also realized that Wayne needed to do it by himself or continue to be teased.

"Move your legs boy, and stop all that flappin'. You got to do dis' on yo' own," he spoke confidently. "Grab hold, and just roll over!"

Instantly the flapping stopped; Wayne rolled over and began moving his arms and legs toward Marvin, arriving safely at the side of the bank.

The nervous silence of the crowd was quickly replaced by roars of applause and hearty slaps on the back from the Duncan clan as he passed, clearly exhausted and thankful.

Embracing Patricia-Ann who was visibly shaken, he took in the words of praise that continued in the background from excited witnesses. Wayne Ivy went into the water the cowardly fat kid, and emerged the courageous victor! He had survived the Giant.

A few of the boys had begun climbing into the tree house and motioned for him to join them. Dripping wet, he proudly headed to take his place among the boys in the clubhouse. He turned and entered, forever new.

There were plenty of stories over the years that caused those listening to roar with laughter, or cry with sadness. Either way, conquer the Giant.

"Whoa that was a good tale. I reckon I'll be next," said the new kid.

"Yep, sho' nuff.

Mattie looked up and noticed Wayne sitting on the ledge outside the clubhouse listening to them tell his story once more. His thick legs were swinging back and forth as he rested against on the old dirty log used to keep the boys from falling out.

"Hey Wayne, how you doin'?" Mattie yelled up.

"I'm doin' fine thank you, how you?"

 "I'm fair I reckon."

"You gonna swing one day yo'self?" he asked curiously.

"Oh yes indeed, but not right ready for that just yet, but one day."

Waving him off she skipped over to rejoin Pamela and the others who were still standing around.

"Hey Pamela, you wanna swing?" yelled one of the children.

"Not today, but thank you for askin'" Pamela responded with envy while Mattie shook her head nervously.

 Mattie glanced over at Pamela, who was enviously watching the children waiting their turn.

"Go on, Pamela, if'n you want. I'll just sit right here and watch. Go 'head!"

"You sure, Mat?"

"I'm sho, 'cause one of these days I'm gonna be swingin'."

"Yep, Mattie that's fo' sho, 'cause I'm gonna teach you to swim and we'll swing together. "

Pamela tapped Mattie lightly on the shoulder and ran to join the other children eagerly waiting their turn.

Mattie sighed and began looking for a comfortable spot to sit; as she leaned against the Giant she began to examine the characteristics of the children standing in line:

Marcus Whitmore, whose nose always seemed to be running.

Tyrone Tyler, whose clothes and shoes never seemed to fit.

Kimberly Hillman, the smartest girl in class and one of the prettiest, who constantly bit her nails.

Keith Lee Smith, always talking, and seeming much older, like he'd been here before.

Then there was Marvin, Gerald, Sandra and Paulette Duncan, who could run faster, jump higher and swim farther than all the kids in the whole county.

Mattie sat for a moment watching, laid her head back, and closed her eyes.

The courtroom was filled with excited anticipation. The surprise witness had begun to cave under the strenuous cross-examination and the spectators began to mumble among themselves. Suddenly the room was filled with the intense sound of the pounding gavel.

"Order in the court, order in the court," yelled the judge sternly. "Attorneys, please approach the bench."

Each approached hurriedly. The attorney for the plaintiff spoke quickly. "Your Honor, I am asking for a mistrial in this case. It is clear that Mr. Marion attacked my client, and he simply acted in self-defense."

"Mr. Washington, do you agree?" the judge asked inquisitively. "Yes, Your Honor, we will drop the charges."

As they returned to their seats the judge looked toward a handsome young man seated quietly, his head down, and hands folded neatly in his lap. "Mr. David Austin, please stand and face the bench, the judge announced loudly, "sir, all charges have been dropped, this is a mistrial." Cheering and sounds of excitement erupted in the courtroom.......

"Mat!....Mattie...Hey dreamer, wake up!" yelled Pamela.

The sounds of children laughing and saying their good-byes echoed in the background. "It's gettin' late, we gotta get home!"

Mattie stood up and stretched.

"Did ya have fun Miss Pamela?" she says, yawning.

"I sho' did, Mat, and I didn't get wet, I landed on the hay bale each time I swung."

"I kin see that." Smiling widely, she picked straws of hay from her hair.

"What did you dream about this time, Mat?"

"I was a lawyer in the big city this time and I helped this young black boy get his daddy free. A white man lied on him so he went to jail, but he was innocent, and this white man said the boy attacked him, but the boy didn't. It is sorta like what they do to some of the black folks here in town. I don't like that."

She stopped and took a deep breath.

"Slow down, Mat....I don't like that either. I'm glad you helped save him, and you know Mattie, one of these days we gon' change the world. You gon' help folks with your gifts and I can't wait to live in the big city, with all the lights and shows. It'll be like heaven."

Pamela stopped, spun around in a circle and kicked her leg high into the air.

"I know you gonna get to go, one of these days Mat."

"We are going to go together and change the world and have lots of jobs, Mat. All of your dreams are gonna come true, and I'm gonna be right there, too. We'll go on all of these great journeys together."

"Yes indeed, we sho will."

Squeezing each other's hands tightly, they continued to skip on down the dirt road. As the approached home, they could see Leona in the distance smiling. They met her at the fork in the driveway. The girls hugged, shook their pinkie fingers and said goodbye.

"I'll see ya in the morning, Mat. Goodnight, Miss Leona," Pamela replied.

"Good night child."

Pamela turned and headed down the driveway, blonde hair blowing gracefully in the wind, while Pauline waved from the porch.

"Yep, I'll see ya tomorrow," said Mattie, solemnly.

Mattie grabbed Leona's hand and squeezed gently.

"Somethin' on your mind, child?" Leona asked lovingly.

"No ma'am, just wonderin' why some folks git things and others don't."

"You know there is a time for everything, Mattie," said Leona tenderly. "It's just not our time, but one day when you least 'spect it, all of your dreams gon' come true. But you must know that if'n you want somethin' bad enough, you just ask for it, believe you gon' get it."

Leona held Mattie's hand tightly as they turned and looked towards home.

"Sumtimes I dream 'bout bein' places, and doin' things for folks but it ain't me, but it is me. Then thangs happen that seem really diff'rent, you know, I can fly all over the place, become diff'rent, and makes me feel like I'm kinda special," she said earnestly. "Do you think sumthin's wrong wit' me?"

Leona gently lifted Mattie's head and stared into her eyes. She was silent a moment, then spoke.

"You've always been a special chil', Mattie Fitch. I knew when you was born that you would do good things, it wuz in yo' eyes from da' moment I seen ya," she said, sighing briefly. "I knew'd you wouldn't be here in Darlington too long, you'd be out there in dis' big ol' world doin' lots of good fo' everybody else," she said lovingly. "You is a special gift, and you gotta do what you wuz sent here to do, can't be no other way."

"I git that feelin' sometimes too, Ma, like I have some-thin' I'm 'posed to do, and one day I'll be shown just what it is." Mattie looked away briefly. "Like I dreamt 'bout Mr. Woods, his wife and son, and I told him bout' it. He seemed right happy when I finished, but I see lots of thangs, and one day I reckon…"

"One thing 'bout time," Leona interrupted. "It'll sho'ly tell us all we need to know when it's ready for us'n to know Mattie, you just wait and see."

All at once a small gust of wind sent a strong smell of Grandma Goldie's chicken frying as they stepped onto the porch, excitement filling them. A crack of lightning followed by a roar of thunder caused them to quickly enter through the squeaking screen door. Another summer storm was preparing to pass over.

Chapter 3
Take the First Swing

With summer in full swing the children were excitedly anticipating the next victim who had mustered up enough courage over the winter months to challenge the Giant.

Pamela had been secretly trying to teach Mattie how to hold her breath using the family's water barrel. Would it prove to be a much easier feat than faring the Giant and the creek?

"Okay, I want you to hold your breath and count each finger, Mat, like this," Pamela flicked her fingers one by one. "And then come up for air, like this here." She pulled her hair back slightly, sucked in a gust of air and plopped her face down into the barrel of water. Mattie, her eyes twitching, began to jump up and down clearly not bothered by the residual water that splashed about.

In the distance, Leona and Dozier were returning home with a fresh corn pie after visiting with old man Woods.

"Look yonder Dozier," said Leona.

"Lawd, what in da' world has them two gon' and dun' naw?" Dozier said sharply.

"Hush fo' a minit." Leona scolded.

They watched with increasing humor.

Mattie grabbed her ponytails, pulled them back tying them in a knot; all at once she reared her head back.

No longer able to contain herself, Leona yelled out just as Mattie prepared to dunk.

"Hey, what y'all doin' by that water barrel?"

Briefly startled, Mattie yelled out excitedly, "Hey Ma and Pa! Pamela's teachin' me how to swim."

"Swim, Mattie? In the barrel, you sho' bout that?" said Leona, in a confused tone. "You best be careful."

"Oh no, Miss Leona, she's just practicin' holdin' her breath to get use to the water," said Pamela quickly.

Dozier, the strong silent type, and often remembered for knocking out a mule, reached down and tapped Leona silently on the hand.

"Mattie Fitch," his voice deep yet comforting.

"Yes sir," said Mattie, eyes smiling lovingly.

"You hear yo' mama, be's careful, ya hear?"

"I will Pa, you gon' watch me fo' a spell?"

"Naw ain't got time, you gon' but I don't 'spect you headin' to dat thar tree no time soon I reckon."

"Oh, no sir Pa, ain't right ready fo' that I don't think."

"All right naw, supper be comin' soon ya hear," Leona interrupted.

"Yes'm."

The girls waved goodbye, smiling mischievously at one another.

"Okay, I'm ready!" Mattie yelled. She looked enthusiastically at Pamela,

her big brown eyes glistening. "I knows I kin do dis' here."

"Hold on naw Mattie, you gotta be right careful," Pamela said.

"Come on naw Pamela, I says I'm ready," says Mattie, slightly irritated.

"I know, I know, I just wanna...."

Suddenly without warning Mattie sucked in a gust of air her cheeks full, threw her face into the barrel so hard that water was propelled everywhere.

Pamela stood stunned.

"Lawd have mercy Mattie Fitch, what cha doin'!," Pamela shouted into the barrel.

Mattie's fingers flicked while Pamela counted down "4-3-2-1, come on Mat!"

Her head came out of the barrel with as much intensity as it had gone in. She energetically wiped away the streams of water that cascaded down her face.

"Oh lordy Pamela, wuz I swimmin'?"

"Mattie, you okay?" says Pamela, grabbing a cloth from her apron and wiping the water from Mattie's face.

"Sho' I'm okay, did ya see me? I'm wuz swimmin'!"

Mattie, excited began to dance around in a circle.

"Come on Pamela, let's do it again cuz befo' you know it, I'm gon' be swimmin' in da creek wit cha, you reckon?"

"Oh no Mattie, it's gon' take a little time but you are doin' just fine," she replied nervously.

"I can't wait to show everybody that I kin swim now. I don't got to sit on the side no mo'. I bet I kin do it now cuz I can hold my breath 'n all," Mattie replied, still flicking water from her hair.

"No Mattie, don't you go nowhere near that swing, 'cause you not ready just yet. It takes a lot more than just holdin' your breath, you have to know how to move your arms 'n kick yo' legs. It's a lot of work 'n you ain't ready yet," said Pamela seriously, grabbing Mattie by the arms and shaking her.

"I knows, I knows," Mattie responded, slightly frustrated.

"I'm serious Mat, you remembers what happened to Wayne last summer. He almost drowned, " said Pamela, looking her square in the eye.

"I hear ya, but I bet it won't take me long," Mattie stated with confidence.

"I'm sure it won't be 'cause you doin' a good job." Pamela was standing, staring with a look of concern.

They inhaled deeply, squatted down, and leaned against the barrel. Neither one spoke.

As the light of day rose slowly, the Fitch household was filled with its normal sound of hummin', and the sweet smell of breakfast cooking in the kitchen, the heart of their home.

Dozier walked into the kitchen wearing his worn blue overalls and dingy white t-shirt.

"I found this here shirt out in the trash barrel. I reckon you don't know how it got there?" He looked over at Leona who was standing at the stove.

"This here is my best, and I just knows my wife wouldn't a put it out thar, now would she?"

"Dozier Lee Fitch, Lordy be, you done gone and found that there shirt again?" Drying her hands on the apron she walked over quickly smacking Dozier on the arm, breaking into a hearty laugh.

"How'd you know?"

"I seent you when you brought the bag out to the shed, and puts it in the bin. Then I waited for you to head back, and I pulled it out," he said, kissing her gently on the forehead.

"Dozier, you worse than the chilren', now sit on down, yo' breakfast is 'bout done."

One by one the Fitch children entered the kitchen, greeted their parents, sat down and prepared to eat. Mattie was always the last to arrive.

"Good mornin' sunshine," Dozier stated happily as she jumped up onto his knee. "Yo' dreams made ya late agin dis' morning, huh?"

"Yes sir Pa, mornin', everyone!" Mattie replied enthusiastically.

She quickly jumped down and skipped over to Leona who had been patiently waiting. After a brief hug and a greeting to her brothers they said grace and began to eat.

"Hey Pa, they burnin' the fields this time of year?" Her eyebrows slightly raised.

"No indeed Mattie, it's not dat time of year. Why you askin'?" Dozier answered with a puzzled tone.

"Well I was wonderin' why the strange red color was out back. It looks like the sun dun' set the moon on fire."

"What you talkin' 'bout, chil'?"

Dozier without hesitation rose quickly and headed out the front door, the rest of the family following close behind. He stepped off the porch and headed toward the rear of the house. Suddenly, they all stood in silent shock and amazement at what they saw in the distance.

There was an uncommonly calm, eerie feeling in the air. The sky was shaded with a strange red tint and the clouds were gathered together like bales of cotton. This caused the hairs on the back of both Dozier and Leona's necks to stand on end.

"It's lookin' a bit peculiar out here, Dozier," Leona stated nervously, met by sounds of agreement from their sons.

"I remember the ol' folks use to say that wasn't a good sign, when the sun tries to burn the moon. Sumthin' bad's gon' happen," Jake stated seriously.

He looked over at the family, and pointed toward the sky.

"You hush chil'. Don't be sayin' sucha thang," Leona replied quickly.

"Yes indeed, that's sho' is what they say," Jay echoed his brother nervously.

"Boys, I think we best be gettin' out to that thar field, and finish up as quickly as we can. Thars a storm or sumpthin' a brewin'," Dozier said firmly. "Let's get to it!"

The boys headed out toward the field and for about ten minutes Dozier was unable to move, standing transfixed staring off into the horizon; an uneasy feeling gnawed in the pit of his stomach, never making it to the field. Mattie walked over and quietly grabbed his hand.

"Pa, sumthin's wrong. I kin feel it too."

"Mattie, don't worries yo'self, but I wants you to stay close to this here house today, ya hear."

Dozier pulled her close to his side, and they stood together watching the sky.

A moment later Leona burst onto the porch, startling both of them.

"Y'all come on now and finish yo' food."

"Lord, woman, you 'bout scared me out my britches!"

"Beg my pardon, but y'all need to come on now we don't got no time to waste."

Mattie tugged lightly on the back of Leona's apron as she turned to enter the house.

"What is it Mattie?"

"Me and Pa gots a bad feelin'. You reckon we right?"

"I prays that all will be well, n' I reckon that's all we kin do right now."

"But y'all said da ol' folks say a red sun's a bad sign. I dreamed sumthin' bad the otha night but dis time I couldn't see who it was. They drowned in the creek."

Mattie, I wants for ya to stay close to dis here house today, you hear me?"

"Yes'm, I will."

As Leona turned and entered the house Mattie stared off one last time, took a deep breath and entered the house. Silence was everywhere.

Leona came out a couple of hours later to take in the laundry, but was pre-occupied with the color in the sky that intensified as the day went on. She hadn't noticed Pamela who walked up and joined her in staring into the sky. After a moment or two she spoke.

"Hey Miss Leona," Pamela asked innocently, startling Leona. "Sumthin' wrong?"

"Oh lord chil' you gave me a fright. All is well. How you?"

"I'm fine. Is Mattie done wit' her chores?"

"I reckon you kin go inside and see if'n she's there, but she should be finished."

"I already did Ms. Leona, but she wasn't there."

"Mattie!" shrieked Leona.

All at once a sickening feeling fell upon Leona, her face tingled and her breathing became labored. There was no answer from Mattie.

"Dozier!, Dozier! Is Mattie wit cha?" she called out nervously towards the field.

Dozier stood up immediately.

"Naw, she's ain't out here," he responded anxiously. "Why, what's da matter?"

" She's not here!"

"Jaycob, run over to her spot and sees if she's a dreamin.'"Dozier ordered.

He headed without delay toward Mattie's dreaming spot, as one by one they dropped their bags and headed towards the house.

Leona stood speechless.

"She ain't here Pa, she ain't!" yelled Jaycob in a panic.

"Dozier, you don't reckon she gone to that tree, do ya?" Leona asked anxiously.

"Come on here boys, sumthin' done happen to yo' sister. Let's git, now!" yelled Dozier.

Instantly, yet quietly, every one of them went into action moving towards the road without hesitation. Pamela had already started moving toward the tree with crazy thoughts racing through her mind as she crossed the road.

"Mattie wouldn't go to the tree. She can't swim. I asked her to wait for me," she pondered.

Unimaginable scenarios played out in everyone's mind like a nightmares. Overwhelmed, Pamela tried to think positive thoughts as the tree began to appear in the distance.

Following closely at the rear were the entire Miles clan right on Pamela's heels.

"Dozier! Oh Lord, please, please," panted Leona, panicking more with every step.

As Dozier listened to the terror in Leona's voice and saw the alarm on the faces of his sons, it was more than he could take. All the strength he possessed left in an instant and his knees began to buckle, but he knew that he was now at the mercy of a source greater than himself.

As Pamela approached the crossing, she could see Mattie swinging back and forth, her smile enormous and wide. By this time everyone had reached the crossing each filled with nervous dread.

Dozier and Leona, out of breath and visibly shaken, approached the tree. Dozier attempted to address Mattie when her eldest brother Michael, grabbed him and motioned for him to see about Leona who had dropped to her knees.

Michael approached slowly and stood adjacent to the Giant close to the edge of the water for a better look at Mattie.

"Now Mattie, you need to git on down from there," he stated calmly, "'cause you know'd you don't know how'ta swim."

"Yes I do Michael 'cause Pamela's been teachin' me!" she yelled, continuing to swing. "I told ya I could do it by myself!"

"Yeah, Mat, but I told ya that you weren't ready to do it by yourself just yet," Pamela responded quickly.

Everyone began looking frantically for an alternative spot that Mattie could land besides the creek. The large hay bale would be the first choice and the easiest but they knew the timing had to be just right—if not, disaster.

"Mattie! You git on down rat now, you givin' Mama a fright!" Michael yelled harshly.

"Mattie Lee Fitch, Lord, chil', you come down off'n dat thar swing, rat now, it ain't safe!" Dozier repeated. "Daniel, run to town and get Doc Adams, hurry!"

By this time the swing was slowing its momentum, leaving her stuck over the creek.

Mattie's confidence level began to dwindle as feelings of nervousness from all of the excitement settled in the eyes of her family. Suddenly, the dream she had a few nights previous entered her consciousness. The face of the drowning person was herself, and now, the once confident child was awakened to the reality. She wanted to jump.

All at once Michael, Dozier and Jaycob moved closer to edge of the creek to try and position them to safely grab her. They were attempting to guide Mattie to a spot where she could potentially release herself from the rope in the shallow end of the creek because without a doubt she was going into the water.

The rest made their way to the base of the Giant, where the ladder to the clubhouse began, and the loop of the rope stuck out of the tree, across from the hay bale.

By this time, her confident smile had turned into an even more nervous grimace. Mattie was, however, more than willing to come down, realizing that she was in trouble the visible signs of concern and worry all around her.

Dozier, determined to remain calm, began to sweat profusely.

"Hey Sunshine, we gon' hold our arms right together and make our way out to get cha, ya hear?" Dozier said, wiping sweat from his brow. "I wants you to come on down off'n the rope right where I tells ya."

"All right pa."

Mattie nodded her head, closed her eyes and smiled widely, catching everyone by surprise. She was holding tightly to the rope while standing on a small piece of wood attached to the bottom of the swing. Trying to get momentum she began moving her knees up and down pulling the rope so she could land on the side.

David had climbed the ladder and was making his way out onto the limb with hopes to grab the rope as Mattie began to move.

"No, Mat!" David screamed, snatching his hand back at just the right moment.

"Wait Mattie, not yet!!!!" yelled everyone in unison.

"NO!!!!! MATTIE!!!!!"

Leona screamed, instantly dropping to her knees.

Dozier and the boys along with Pamela jumped into the creek.

"Lord have mercy, grab her!" Leona panicked.

Michael reached Mattie first, who was floating face down. Grabbing her by the dress, he continued to slip on the creek bottom as he tried unsuccessfully to turn her over.

Finally, still fighting to hold on to Mattie's dress, he reached over and took a hold of her ponytail, as Dozier pushed up from underneath keeping their heads above water. With one final tug he turned her over.

"I got her!" Dozier grunted, still struggling to stand on the slippery bottom.

"I gotcha Pa, hang on to her," roared Michael."

"Mattie!" Dozier screamed, trying to get out of the water.

"David, fetch that stick over yonder!" Leona shouted, pointing toward the tree.

David ran, grabbed the stick and hurried over to assist Dozier who had linked himself with Jaycob.

By this time Daniel and Doc Adams arrived with a few of the elders who had been at the store when Daniel ran up. A couple of the men rushed over to try and be of assistance to the Fitch men.

Lonnie and Pauline had come outside to call Pamela in when all of a sudden old man Woods ran up, breathless and panicked.

"Lord have mercy, the child's done fell in the creek. You betta get on over there. It's Miss Mattie!"

Pauline stood motionless.

Lonnie, without stopping for his next thought, headed for the tree.

In one fell swoop the men were able to pull Dozier, Michael and Mattie onto the edge of the creek. Suddenly, there was an eerie silence that fell upon the crowd. Everyone stood dazed and confused, Mattie was unresponsive.

"How'd this happened to little Miss Mattie?" whispered one of the spectators.

Lonnie pressed his way through the crowd to Leona, who was visibly distraught. Doc began address Mattie's head wound, as she was unconscious.

The troubled women stood quietly praying, while the townsmen attempted to console them.

"Pick her up, Dozier," Doc Adams ordered. "Let's get her to the house."

Dozier, still numb, wiped his face and pushed back his hair, which was still drizzling water. He walked slowly over to Mattie's unconscious body and in an instant flashed back over her twelve years. He squatted down, picked her up and kissed her lightly on the forehead.

"I love you, Sunflower," he whispered. "Pa's here."

The women along with the rest of the Fitch family and everyone who had been standing around followed close behind. No one spoke a word.

Then, out of nowhere, the crowd began to sing.

"This little light of mine, I'm gonna let it shine oh, this little light of mine, I'm gonna let it shine." It was Mattie's favorite song.

Pauline looked over at Pamela, who was an emotional wreck, and smiled a loving smile, one of those I'm-trying-to-keep-from-looking-distressed smiles. Pamela returned the sentiment with a grin while small tears flowed quietly down her cheeks.

The walk to the Fitch's house seemed a little longer than usual.

"Doc, you reckon she gon' be all right?" Dozier asked softly.

"Once we get her inside I kin check more, but right now I can't say."

They entered the house and walked into her room and placed her gently atop the bed. Doc Adams stepped over to her, looking disheartened. He pulled out his stethoscope, placing it gently on Mattie's chest, and began to check her over.

"She is breathing right fine and her heart sounds strong," looking over his shoulder to the family. "But she's in a deep sleep, and she'll wake up when she's ready." He stood up and walked over to Dozier and Leona, standing at the foot of the bed.

"Rest is the most important thing right now, not too much noise, and lots of love," he stated in a whisper. "I'll come round an check in ta-morrow."

"It's my fault," Pamela said, sobbing uncontrollably. "If I had just taught her some more, I'm sorry."

Leona's voice was trembling as she looked around the room at the Miles', blameless.

"Hush now, you haven't done one thang wrong," Leona stated, lovingly her voice trembling. "Mattie is strong in mind and spirit, and God's got this one, ya hear?"

"Much obliged Doc, and we'll be getting' some pay for ya," Dozier said humbly.

"No sir, we'll take care of that, Dozier," Lonnie said interrupting.

"Well all right, we kin worry bout that later. Lemme know if there be any changes," Doc said, gathering his things, I'll be round."

Dozier and Lonnie escorted him to the door, and watched silently as he walked down the path crowded with the inquisitive onlookers.

"Not much we kin do right naw 'cept pray." Dozier beckoned to the crowd that had gathered outside.

Back inside where the family was assembled, Leona moaned, "We have ta be quiet now. She gon' rest awhile I reckon. Come on say goodnight, y'all."

Quietly as they could, each one came and whispered in Mattie's ear, lightly kissing her forehead and cheek. In a sigh, Leona and Dozier whispered, "Dream, Mattie Fitch, dream."

Mattie squeezed Dozier's hand, but never moved.

She slept.

Chapter 4
The Inner City

The sound of a shotgun rang out in the distance, sending those within an earshot scrambling to find a safe refuge, and determined not to become an innocent victim of the rage that plagued their neighborhood. Moments later the sound of sirens allowed those with enough nerve to emerge.

Loiterers gathered in front of liquor stores as the abandoned buildings on every other street corner stood covered with graffiti. Peering through cold black security gates were the faces of the children and elderly too afraid to go out into the streets of the place they once called beautiful. The people living along the avenues were hard-working folks, most of them having lived in the city for many years while searching for the good life. Drugs had infiltrated the inner structure, causing the residents to live in fear. What they once had called home was giving way to the influx of gangs and drug dealers. There was no peace anywhere in the everyday life of the residents of the Triangle. Night fell, and the people hid.

One street in particular was Beacon Lane, where Marion and Margaret Lovell had resided for the past twenty years. They had not been able to have children, but many of the children in the neighborhood spent hours with the Lovells. Mrs. Lovell, a teacher and Mr. Lovell, a city worker, were stand-in parents to many who were without a solid family structure, becoming instrumental in saving numerous lives. The Lovells were a mature couple, looking forward to retirement and spending their golden years filled with peace and happiness. However, much to their surprise, Margaret became pregnant with a baby girl, whom they named Angel.

Marion had been the strength of the family. He was a loving, spiritual husband and nurturing father, who died 3 months shy of Angel's sixteenth birthday. Margaret had given birth to Angel later in life, and the stress of having to work two jobs took its toll on her physically; she started to fall ill. However, she continued to press forward, standing on the promise that she had made to her husband. She was determined not to lose her daughter to the streets.

Angel, affectionately known as Princess to her parents, was a petite, beautiful young woman, with flawless mahogany skin. She had the best of everything. She was both a mommy's and a daddy's girl often teased and called church girl. She was a good student with dreams of getting out of the 'hood, but her taste for the wild side of life would eventually be sated.

Marcus a well-known gangster in the 'hood, had his eyes on Angel, and whatever he wanted, he got. His deep dimples emerged in unison with a smile of flawless white teeth, he was (always?) perfectly dressed and he did not want for anything. He was an angry young man—and rightfully so. At the age of ten he witnessed the murder of his father, a Good Samaritan who had attempted to intervene in a robbery at the local gas station. As he grew Marcus became angrier and settled into the notion that revenge would someday be his redemption.

He began to question everything that he had been taught, eventually making choices that would create chaos in a life where calm should have dwelled, with an outcome that would be life-altering.

Marcus would often tease and taunt Angel as she and her group of friends walked home from school in the afternoon. There was something special about her, a connection that he felt when she walked by. The innocence of her smile and the beauty of her eye 'caused him to forget the harshness of the lifestyle he had chosen.

He stood confidently waiting for his friends to arrive to their meeting spot in front of the store, when he saw Angel and her group of girlfriends apoproaching.

"Hey pretty girl, come here," asked Marcus loudly.

"Who you talkin' to?" yelled her friend Annette, "We all look good."

This brought laughs from the girls.

"She knows who I'm talking to, right Angel?"

He licked his lips and blew her a kiss.

"What you want?" she replied, "I got things to do."

"Like what, go home and get in them books you carrying?" Marcus teased.

He slowly approached, reached out his hand softly biting his lower lip. "Let me see what you learnin'."

"I have to get home. Maybe another time," said Angel nervously, quickly pulling away.

"Wait a minute," he said, grinning as he tried unsuccessfully to grab her arm. As he leaned into her ear he whispered both slowly and seriously, "One of these days you will be mine."

Angel tried, unsuccessfully, not to make eye contact. The scent of his cologne was overwhelming; his shoulders were broad, and his arms were muscular. She just stared for what seemed like a lifetime.

"You have beautiful eyes," she said innocently.

These words caught him by surprise, leaving him speechless. He cleared his throat, backed away, putting his hand out giving them permission to pass.

"You ought to give me those digits before you go," he said pleasantly.

"777-93-11," Angel said jokingly.

"Oh you got jokes," said Marcus clearly intrigued by her feistiness.

"I was just kidding. Why you so serious?" she said.

They exchanged a brief stare and smile.

"Are you gon' give me the number or not?" Marcus replied, saucily.

"It's 555-2812, and I gotta go now," Angel stated arrogantly.

"Yeah, okay pretty girl," yelled Marcus, laughing. "Nine o'clock."

There was complete silence as the girls walked down the street. Then Kris spoke up.

"Angel, I know you are not gon' mess with Marcus. Girl, your mama will kill you."

"Girl, I can't help it. He is fine, you got to admit that," said Angel, with a note of excitement in her voice.

"You right about that, but he is still bad news," said Annette, grabbing her arm. "He looks good, but he is trouble."

"I won't mess with him--stop trippin'--but I can look," she said slyly.

Headed into the apartment complex she turned and took one final glance back to see if her intuition was right.

"Yep he's lookin'. I knew it."

"Oh yeah he's gonna look girl till he gets in them panties!" Annette replied sarcastically.

"Girl be smart, and besides you to good for him." Kris added firmly.

"Well I gotta go in. I'll check y'all later."

"Bye" they responded in unison.

There was a strong chemistry between them. Angel was clearly aware of the pain and disappointment her choice would place on her mother. However, she was unable to control the urge that compelled her toward him.

"Where are you going, Angel? I'm a little tired tonight and not feeling my best," asked Margaret, her voice shaking between coughs.

"Just right outside for a little while, Mother," Angel said, frowning.

She began to pace back and forth impatiently slowly making her move toward the door.

"But it's getting late, Princess" said Margaret in a whisper.

"I'm going to be just out front for a minute then I'll be right back," Angel stated firmly.

She turned and quickly headed out the door before Margaret had time to respond.

Margaret knew deep down that something wasn't right. Angel had never been secretive with her before. She walked to the window gently pulling back the corner of her perfectly ironed drapes; she gazed out into the dusk to see Angel standing in the distance. After a deep breath of air she looked up, shook her head gently and gave thanks." There was nothing else she could do.

In a short period of time the relationship between Angel and Marcus seemed to flourish. Margaret refused to isolate her daughter, but Marcus seemed to have a control over Angel that was hard to break.

Angel came in from school a bit late and joined her mother at the kitchen table and nervously cleared her throat.

"Precious, is there something wrong with you? Are you sick?" Margaret asked uneasily.

"What are you talking about?" Angel replied in a surprised tone.

Frustrated, Angel scooted away from the table putting a small distance between them. Angel couldn't figure out how her mom knew.

"Are you pregnant, child?"

There were a few moments of silence.

"I don't know what to say. I can't hide it anymore. Yeah I'm pregnant."

Margaret's worst nightmare had come true.

The Birth

Marcus Freeman, Jr. was a beautiful baby boy with big brown eyes and curly locks of hair. They nicknamed him Deuce. He was a treasure, and his birth had given them all a sense of peace and closeness. Marcus Sr. worked hard trying to provide a legal way of life for all of them. But staying clean would prove to be a difficult task.

"Girl, you don't understand. I am looking for a job, and they won't cut a brother no slack!" he yelled.

Well you just have to keep lookin,' something will show up. You got to have faith that things will work out. We have a son to raise!"

"You think I don't know that, girl? I'm doing the best I can with what I know!" he responded, frustrated.

The pain and disappointment weighed on him. And going back to jail was not something he desired; however caring for Deuce and Angel were his first priority, at any cost.

Maybe if I can do just one more drop, he thought.

Marcus figured that he could do one final delivery that would secure enough money to get them out of the neighborhood for good. He had been able to elude the police most of his life. Just one more time.

It took him a few days to set everything up. This time things felt a little off to him. He had a bad feeling. The closer the time, the worse he felt, hearing Angel's voice ringing in his ears.

It was time to go. All of a sudden the vibration of his cell phone caught him off guard.

"Hey what's up?" He answered abruptly.

"Where you at baby? I been calling for over an hour." Angel asked nervously.

"I got somethin' to do. I'll get back to you later."

The sound of Deuce in the background gave him chills. He stood on the sidewalk watching the crew get into the car as visions of his father entered his mind, and the thought of going to jail shook him. He couldn't do it.

"What up, Marcus?" said one of the crew. "Let's go!"

After a moment he turned and began walking slowly down the street.

"Marcus, hey nigga, what up?"

He never looked back.

"Hey, what you doin' sittin' out here by yourself?" Marcus asked humbly.

"Oh my goodness, I thought something had happened to you." Angel replied with excitement.

She rose quickly and grabbed him around the neck kissing him repeatedly.

"Okay baby I'm home, I'm cool. Where's Deuce?"

"Inside with Mama. I am not sure what was going down but I am glad you didn't go and that's all I'm gonna say."

"Yeah, like you said Angel, things are gonna get better."

A few hours later they were awokened by a pounding on the frontdoor. Marcus jumped to his feet and headed to the door only to be greeted by several cops flashing guns.

"We got you this time Marcus ain't no getting' away."

Two of the 5 policeman grabbed him, spun him around and began handcuffing and reading his rights.

"What are you doing, too him. Marcus!" Angel yelled from the hallway.

"Just go back baby we know I didn't do anything so don't worry."

Marcus' arrest came as a shock, but they were confident that he would be cleared of any charges he had a tight alibi. That was not the case.

"We, the jury, find the Defendant, Marcus Freeman, Sr., guilty of felony armed robbery!"

Gasps and sobs erupted from Angel as Margaret tried unsuccessfully to console her. They were confident he would be found innocent.

"Man, I'm innocent!" screamed Marcus. He looked toward the jury in shock. "You gotta be kidding me! I'm innocent! For once in my life I'm innocent!"

Deuce, who had been sleeping began screaming for his father.

"Order in this courtroom!" shouted the judge, pounding his gavel. "Everyone sit down and come to order!"

The judge motioned for the bailiffs to restore order.

The sounds of mumbling and whispering taking place throughout the audience became muffled as the bailiffs scrambled to resume order.

"Mr. Freeman, please rise," the judge ordered. "This court has found you guilty and based upon your past criminal history be happy I'm not throwing the book at you. You are hereby sentenced to fifteen years with the possibility of parole after 10. So it is up to you Sir, to decide when you are released."

Marcus plopped down in his seat visibly in a state of shock. He turned and looked at Angel who was crying uncontrollably.

"I'm so sorry," he mouthed. "I love you. Take care of my son."

His eyes began filling with tears. Marcus flashed back to his father.

"I'm going to ask for an appeal, Mr. Freeman. Please don't lose hope. I'll contact you in a couple of weeks." The attorney patted Marcus on the back and began gathering his things.

"Thank you." Marcus responded quietly his voice trembling and visibly broken. "Don't worry, man, this is for all the stuff I did and never got caught for. Do what you can, but just make sure my girl and son are okay."

As the guards approached, he stood, preparing to be shackled.

"Take care of my son." Marcus yelled to Angel. "Get him out of here, Angel. I don't want him to see me like this!"

"Daddy!" Deuce whimpered innocently.

Angel and Margaret gathered Deuce, quickly ushering him out of the door as he reached back over her shoulder toward Marcus.

"Mommy, my daddy!"

"Deuce please! Daddy's got to go away for awhile."

Angel, crying and confused, exited the courtroom looking around frantically for a place to sit and gather her thoughts. Margaret reentered the courtroom and walked over to Marcus who was being handcuffed.

"I want you not to worry about Angel and Marcus. We will be fine and work to bring you home."

"Thanks Ma, I appreciate that, and thanks for believing in me."

"Let's go!" ordered the bailiff.

Their eyes met one last time.

"Be strong, keep your head up!" Margaret yelled down the hall.

Marcus nodded.

Five Years

"Deuce, what would you like to be when you finish school?" asked Margaret, as they sat around the table preparing to eat dinner. "You are eleven years old now, and pretty soon you will be going off to college."

Angel giggled as she placed the dinner plates on the table.

"Mama, he's only eleven. Good grief."

"Well the child's gotta be ready."

"Ummm. I think I'm gonna to be a lawyer," he said confidently, "so I can get my daddy outta jail, because he is innocent."

Margaret and Angel, both stunned, sat in total silence at the response of such a young child.

"Well Deuce, that will be a great accomplishment for you to achieve, and if anyone can do it, you can," Angel smiled in admiration.

The years that followed would not be kind. Marcus grew more and more bewildered and angry. He refused their visits, telling Angel not to bring Deuce to prison to see him. Eventually she stopped visiting, but never ceased writing or working on getting her husband out of prison.

It was a cold rainy day, right around Easter. Deuce and Margaret had been coloring eggs for the children in the neighborhood. This had become an annual event, and all the kids looked forward to going to Miss Margaret's for a day filled with activities. This day was different.

Margaret had not been well since Marion died. Sadness had become her companion, but faith was her stronghold. By the time Deuce was born, her health was not the same, but the smile on his face gave her the strength to go one more day.

Deuce never wanted to disappoint Margaret, so he strove to do his best in school, excelling in all of his classes. He was a genius. Fulfilling his promise to stay out of trouble and become an attorney was always at the forefront of his mind. He had been able to stay out of trouble because Margaret was there to keep him focused. The problem was his peers who nicknamed him "schoolboy", which he hated. But she was always there to tell him firmly to remember what his purpose was, and remind him, "don't be troubled by troublemakers, 'cause you are fully responsible for your actions and don't allow yourself to be influenced by others."

"One day I am gonna take care of you and my mama and we'll move wherever you like, okay?" he stated with a touch of innocence.

"That sounds good, Deuce. Can we move to Hawaii?"

"Anywhere you want."

He would learn many things from Margaret during their late night talks, while Angel worked and attended school. They would sit in the kitchen and drink cups of hot chocolate, his favorite, while she shared stories of her childhood growing up in the South. Deuce was intrigued by her life and thought she was the smartest and wisest woman in the world. After a while it would become apparent to him that something was very wrong with his grandmother. She was no longer able to hide the inevitable.

"Grandma, what's wrong? You don't look so good." Deuce asked while helping her up from her favorite seat.

"Oh baby, nothing is wrong, Grandma is just not feeling too well today, but don't you worry. If anything ever happens to me you will be taken care of."

She reached over and rubbed his arm, smiling subtlely.

"What do you mean if somethin' happens?"

"Help me up," she said, struggling to catch her breath.

Grabbing her gently by the arm they made their way slowly into the living room and over to her favorite rocking chair as they looked out into the darkness of the street.

"Marcus," she never called him that. "You must always stay focused. The streets are tough and filled with wolves disguised as sheep. They know who easy prey is. You have got to be careful so that you don't end up in the same predicament as your father."

"Aw, don't worry Ma, I'm gonna be just fine. And besides, I am going to be a lawyer, if it's the last thing I do. I promised you and my dad." He laughed nervously. "Besides you talk like you ain't gon' be around."

"*Ain't*, Deuce, *Ain't*? After all that you have been taught, you say 'ain't gon'e' child? There is no way I can go any-where and leave you to spoil all that I have taught you."

She leaned over and tapped him lightly on the arm, causing them both to laugh heartily.

"Aw Grandma, I'm sorry, but sometimes it is so much easier just to say it the way everyone else says it and not worry about all the extra stuff," Deuce stared out in to the night. "It's almost like I live a double life. People expect me to be like my dad was. You know, out there dealin' drugs and fightin' folks. But when I don't live up to that, they think that I'm a punk, and that's one thing I'm not!"

Deuce began to pace back and forth in front of the window at the thought of being harassed.

"Marcus!" Margaret shouted. "Sit down, boy. What is wrong with you? Stop talkin' like that! Oh, Lord help me!"

"Grandma!"

Moments later the sound of sirens would ring in his ears, and the pain in his heart would be more than he could bear.

"Man, what is taking them so long?" Deuce said. "Hospitals stink."

Unable to sit still, Deuce paced back and forth in the waiting room as they prepared to hear the news on Margaret's condition.

"Just wait a minute Deuce. Please sit down. They'll let us know something pretty soon. I can't believe this is happening," Angel moaned. She walked over to the window and looked listlessly down into the parking lot, lost in memories. Suddenly there was a heaviness that overtook them as the doctor entered the waiting room.

"Miss Freeman? Hello I'm Doctor Roberts, I'm very sorry, but we did all that we could do."

"What do you mean?" Angel responded, grabbing Deuce by the arm.

"She is holding on right now, but I'm not sure how much longer she can. Please follow me."

"Oh God, please!"

In shock, they sat for a moment trying to regain their composure.

"Would you like a moment?" asked the doctor, sympathetically.

"Yes, just give us a minute, man. Please," said Deuce impatiently. "Come on Ma, we can do this," he said firmly.

They rose apprehensively and walked out into the hallway of the hospital, and stood in brief silence.

"I can't do this, Deuce," Angel said, breathless. "I'm feeling sick."

"Yes we can. We'll do it together."

"Right this way," motioned the nurse.

The walk to Margaret's room seemed to take forever. Approaching slowly, Angel slowed and leaned against the wall preparing to enter the room.

It felt cold, and the smell was uncommon.

"Is this what death smells like?" Deuce thought.

There was an overwhelming feeling of despair as they entered the room. He stepped forward, approaching her bedside slowly, as Angel stood in the background trying to regain her composure.

Margaret looked unusually peaceful and beautiful, both Deuce and Angel thought, so the idea that she was not going to make it was more than they could comprehend.

He looked anxiously at the nurse who was standing next to the bed.

"Can she hear me?"

"Yes, she can hear you. She may not answer, but she can squeeze your hand if you give it to her," said the nurse, both carefully and sympathetically. "She may be cold, but that's normal," she mouthed.

Leaning down, Deuce kissed her on the cheek. Her face was strangely warm, considering the nurse said she would be cold. She smelled sweet, like lavender. He loved when she wore that fragrance or had it simmering in a pot in the house.

"Grandma, can you hear me?" He whispered. "It's me--Deuce, please don't leave us, don't leave please," he murmured.

The room was quiet.

He sat down on the bed and picked up her warm, but moist hand, awaiting a response, anything. Suddenly she squeezed his hand. Looking up excitedly, Margaret's eyes were open.

"Deuce, Angel," she whispered weakly, "come here."

Angel rushed to her side, laying her ear against Margaret's face, "Mama, I'm here," Angel sighed. Her tears ran unchecked down her cheeks and onto her mother's face as she whispered, "I love you."

"I love you child. Do what you have set out to do," grunted Margaret breathlessly.

"I will," she said, looking despairingly at Deuce, who was beginning to shake.

"Deuce……………..Deuce" Margaret said gasping.

"Yes Grandma, I'm here," he said frantically.

"I love you. Don't forget you have a purpose. I'll always be there. Be a good boy and stay out of trouble."

"I will Grandma, I promise."

"Oh, I'm tired. I'm gonna rest now."

Margaret inhaled a long deep breath. They all stood watching and waiting for the exhale, but it never came.

Goodbye would last forever.

There was a strange feeling in the air, and an odd coloring in the sky. Most of the people did not even seem to notice, it was just another day on the block. Everyone was in a hurry trying to get their business done and get off the streets. Deuce was headed to meet his friends at the corner market where they would gather and do nothing. They were determined to try and stay out of trouble, but trouble was always a street away.

Arriving a few minutes early, he stood watching and analyzing his neighborhood. He thought, "How did I end up here?"

At 17, he knew that his dreams might not become reality, and the chances of college were slim. He could hear the sound of his grandmother's voice, "Deuce, you have a purpose." He missed her deeply; she was the glue that held them together. Angel was working two jobs and trying to finish her last few months of school, leaving him to be responsible, but that was not an easy task.

He turned toward the sounds of laughter, giving his attention to a group of children playing by a broken fire hydrant that spewed just enough water to offer a welcome relief from the heat. The laughter of the children made him smile, as he remembered how much happiness those days used to bring him. There were street vendors along the sidewalks selling their wares, some with pushcarts adorned with half-torn labels and misspelled words.

Deuce leaned against the side wall of the market, his hands placed in the pockets of his pants that rested perfectly on his hips. "Boy, you keep your pants up. It's a sin and a shame that the young men are showin' their underwear and being disrespectful." The voice of his grandmother rang in his mind daily, keeping him constantly focused on his appearance and attitude.

Deuce was a medium built, fine-looking young man. His piercing brown eyes were hypnotizing. Perfectly white teeth gave accent to an electrifying smile that could light up a room. His skin was smooth, like velvet. He was very meticulous about the way he dressed and careful to maintain a well-groomed appearance.

"Hey Deuce, you gon' do great things, if you stay off that corner. That's what got your daddy in trouble. And them gangsters be lookin' for you youngsters to run jobs for 'em," yelled Mr. Walker from the stoop of Preacher's Barbershop.

"Hey Mr. Walker, what's up?" Deuce yelled.

"Come here, boy," motioned another one of the men.

"Y'all leave that boy alone. He already knows that if his Momma tells me anything I'm gonna crack his head," Preacher yelled from the back of the shop. "I promised his grandma that I was gon' be lookin' out for this boy."

"Oh yeah, we got yo' back boy, 'cause one thing we can say, you and your friends seem to have a little bit of sense."

"Hey, boy, how is them books doin'?" asked Preacher.

"Oh I'm doin' real good, still gettin' them A's and still gettin' teased."

"Hey, don't you give them hardheads no time, you go and get yo' game played for real, and make yo' mama and grandma's memory proud, you hear me," spoke another one of the men.

"I know," replied Deuce quickly. "I'm gettin' lots of letters from too many colleges. I don't know which one to choose, but me and my mom's been talking about it. I won't disappoint my family and folks that have been lookin' out for me, that's fo' sho'."

"That's what I'm talkin' about, youngster," Preacher nodded.

"Well I gotta go and meet my boys by the market, I'll see you tomorrow Preacher."

"All right boy, be on time."

Walking back down to the market he continued to take in his surroundings and the thought of having more. He laid his head back against the wall and imagined that life.

"Hey, what's up, fool? Wake up!" yelled one of his friends, as they approached Deuce who had been in deep thought.

"Hey what's up? What took you guys so long?" You know my moms is gon' be lookin' for me in a minute!"

"Hey look, perfect timing," said one of the fellas, pointing toward a group of young ladies headed in their direction.

"Hey, how you doin' big booty?" said Deuce's best friend, Rashad, causing a roar of laughter.

"Man, you don't talk to women that way! What you doin'?" Deuce interjected quickly.

He turned away from the group and smiled slyly at the girls.

"How you doin' today?"

"Whatever Deuce," spoke one young lady as she rolled her eyes and cocked her head.

"See man, that's the reason I don't hang out wit y'all, always messin' up my flow."

"Whatever, fool. You always tryin' to make somebody look bad."

There was complete silence in the group as they watched the girls disappear down the street.

"Man, them church girls are the hardest to get at, but the ones you wanna take home."

"I know, my moms and granny would always tell me how ladies oughta be treated, and they would kill me if I disrespected one," Deuce stated confidently.

"Whatever, dude. Girls is girls, and some don't deserve no respect, you feel me?" said Adrian arrogantly, turning and slapping high-five with Jamal.

"All I know is, if I did something wrong to a girl or lady or somethin', my grandmother would probably come back from the grave and thump me on my head."

In his best falsetto voice Jamal responded:

"I know you right. I could hear your Granny now she would say Marcus, you talking about her big booty!"

The laughter continued for several minutes, and then tediousness set in again.

"I'm bored, man," snubbed Rashad.

"Hey, what else is new?"

The boys made their way slowly to the bus stop. Bored, they began daring one another to sit inside the bus stop overhang where everything reeked of urine.

"That's what I'm gon' have one day boy. I ain't lying!" said Jamal enviously as one of the drug dealers drove by in his Mercedes Benz, his music blasting.

"Yeah, and you'll end up dead or in jail, you better know that," said Rashad snickering, "but I'll drive it for you when you gone."

Clearly frustrated at his futile attempts to keep his crew out of trouble, Deuce spoke hastily.

"You can call me when you get arrested and I'll do what I can to get you out of jail, pro bono." He popped his collar and spun around striking a pose like Michael Jackson, which brought laughter to them all.

"Man, we have made it this far without givin' into that life. It must mean we can get out of here and do somethin' positive!"

"And where are we supposed to go, dude? Off to college, and be some big shot lawyer like you, huh?" said Jamal, irritated. "Let me tell you, Deuce. You ain't goin' nowhere, 'cause yo' granny passed away. Sorry for that. But yo' momma ain't got no money, yo' daddy is in the pen, and you don't have what it takes to get in college."

No one laughed; there was a hush in the group. Deuce took a deep breath, staring confusedly at his friend.

"Man, I'm sorry you think that way, and maybe you're right, but I know this can't be all that there is," he hissed.

The sound of something familiar approaching got their attention.

It was "Two-Strikes," a well-known dealer in the neighborhood. He pulled over to where the boys were standing and rolled down the eerily dark-tinted windows, and motioned for them to walk over. Hesitating, Jamal looked back at Deuce, who was shaking his head in disagreement. They knew he had a job, and each of them had been able to elude him, but he did not like being told no.

"You can go over there and talk to him if you want to," Deuce stated, seriously.

At that moment, he turned to notice an elderly lady walking with a cart filled with groceries, "but you'll end up regrettin' it," he said impatiently. Turning, he fixed his attention back on the woman.

His friends walked over to the car while Deuce stood there, alone and frustrated. The peer pressure was heavy so against his better judgment he walked over to the car.

The elderly lady was interesting looking, not like most, which kept his attention. He couldn't stop staring because he knew most of the people in the neighborhood and he had not seen her before. Her brown eyes were big and beautiful, her skin dark and slightly wrinkled. She was smiling to herself. Her cream-colored dress was covered by a lace apron tied into a bow, and a beautiful multicolored scarf tied loosely under her chin that protected two braids pinned crossways behind each ear, which lifted slightly in the cool breeze.

"Oh Lord, help me please!" yelled the elderly woman, who was losing her step.

Everyone in the group, except Deuce, burst into laughter as the cart gave way and the items spilled into the street.

"Come on, man. Let's help her!" Deuce yelled as he ran over to give his assistance.

"Naw man, you got it!" bellowed Adrian. "We got to make some money."

"Let's do this, fools!" Two-Strikes said impatiently, motioning for the boys to get in the backseat.

Deuce turned back toward the old woman who was carefully picking up the items while he watched in disappointment as they sped away.

"I'll see you when you get out of jail, punk!" he shouted in frustration.

A strange feeling came over him as he approached the woman. The faint sound of his grandmother's voice played over in his head that he had made the right decision. He missed her so much.

"Ma'am, are you all right?" Deuce asked politely, "Please excuse my friends."

He began helping to pick up the last few items still tossed about.

"Oh, yes, I'm all right. Thank you so much," she replied breathless. "And don't you worry, your friends will learn one day," smiling lovingly she touched his hand gently, which caused him to lose his breath, but he shook it off.

Clearing his throat, he responded both quietly and nervously, "I've never seen you around here before. Where do you live?"

"I just moved into that building right there a few days ago and just in the nick of time, I must say," smiling as if she knew him.

"That's where I live too. Where you from?" Deuce stated curiously.

"I am from Darlington, South Carolina. What is your name, young man?"

"Deuce," he answered quickly.

"No, son, what is the name you were born with?" she replied, smiling sweetly.

"Oh, Marcus J. Freeman, Jr." he stated confidently. "But everyone calls me Deuce."

"Well Deuce, my name is Mattie Lee Fitch, but everyone calls me Mattie."

As they headed across the busy intersection toward the apartment complex she reached towards him, locking arms. In the distance Deuce could see a couple of his other friends waving and laughing. He smiled to himself and chuckled.

"Here we are," Mattie sang in a falsetto voice. "Thank you, my dear."

"You live here?" Deuce asked with confused, concern clouding his voice. I thought this was the storage room."

"Oh no, it's more than enough room for me. I don't need much. And thank you for your help," Mattie stated. "Here they are!" wiggling her keys and preparing to unlock the door.

"Umm, you're welcome" he mumbled peeking around her to get a look inside.

The room was spotless. There was a subtle aroma of lavender. In one corner sat a small wooden table with two chairs. Atop the table a bluish colored vase was filled with a bouquet of sunflowers perfectly placed, and an old brass teacup. On the other side of the room, against the wall, was a small wooden framed bed with a beautiful, neatly folded, handwoven quilt. An old black two-burner stove sat directly in the middle with a silver teakettle on top. An overwhelming, mysterious energy gripped him. He was mesmerized.

"Would you like to come on in for a spell, Deuce?" Mattie asked pleasantly, while removing her scarf and shawl.

"Umm, no thanks, I gotta go, lady. I mean Miss Mattie," He said quickly. "You're cool now anyway, but you need to be careful around here. It can get pretty crazy."

"Oh I'm not worried, Deuce. I have you now, and anytime you need me, you come on by."

Mattie smiled pleasantly, as she closed the door.

Deuce stood outside motionless.

He walked out to the sidewalk and looked around for any sign of his friends. It was quiet everywhere except his stomach, so home was his destination.

As he sat on his bed looking out into the darkness longing for his grandmother, he heard what sounded like someone sweeping, followed by the faint sounds of singing.

"This little light of mine, I'm gonna let it shine, Oh, this little light of mine, I'm gonna let it shine."

Sitting up, he held his breath and listened. He opened the window and leaned out, placing his hands securely on the ledge. A cold gush of the night air sent a chill through him, and he closed the window.

Who in the world would be outside this time of the night, in this neighborhood? They would have to be crazy. Slipping on his sneakers, he got up and quietly headed out, tiptoeing down the hallway past his mother's room. He peered in to make sure she was sleeping.

Easing his way to the door, he grabbed the doorknob and turned it slowly, praying that it would not squeak. He looked out into the hallway; it was cold and dark with an eerie feel to it. But the singing drew him, and he felt compelled to check it out. Creeping slowly out into the hall and down each step, the sounds seemed to get closer and closer.

He paused for a moment.

Sliding along the wall, he finally made it to the bottom of the stairs and stood still, breathing deeply. Stepping down, he grabbed the edge of the wall hoping to take a peek without being seen. It was truly not what he had expected to see.

"Miss Mattie, is that you?" he asked, puzzled.

"Well hello, Deuce. How are you?" she asked sweetly.

"What are you doing out here? It's dangerous Miss Mattie," he whispered. "Well, I had this dream, which I do a lot, you know. You see, there was a child crying and he was lonely. I reckon someone had passed and he needed to talk in order to keep himself outta trouble," she said lovingly. "So I knew the best thang to do was come on outdoors here where, if'n there was somebody who needed me, I would be right here available to 'em. You in need of something, Marcus Freeman, Jr.?"

Mattie looked at him over the top of her glasses, as if she had a secret.

"No, I'm cool. I was just checkin' to see what the singin' was," he stated nervously.

Mattie continued to sweep and hum aloud. Out of the corner of her eye, she could see Deuce pacing anxiously.

"Is somethin' on your mind, child?" she asked. "Why don't you come in out of the cold and sit a spell, have somethin' hot to drink?" She walked to the door, opened it slowly and nodded her head in his direction.

"Maybe just for a minute, Miss Mattie, 'cause if my mom's wakes up, it's over for me. But it is a little cold out here."

This will give me a chance to get a better look inside, he thought.

Mattie smiled.

The room was immaculate. Her home was exactly how he had imagined; everything was in its proper place.

All at once he was overcome by the lavender that brought back memories of his grandmother.

"Man, Miss Mattie, that smells just like my grand-mother," he said solemnly.

"Well, I hope that it brings you sweet memories," she answered.

There was an overwhelming sense of a calm and comfort. It was like home.

"Make yourself at home, child" said Mattie, walking over to the cupboard and grabbing two tea cups from the shelf.

"Tell me a little bit about you," said Mattie, enthusiastically. "What do you do? Are you in school? What grade are you in? Am I talking too fast for ya child? Everyone use to tell me that," she said handing him a cup. "Well," she asked impatiently, "I'm waiting."

"Oh okay, well you know my name and all, but I'm seventeen about to be eighteen on December nineteenth.

I'm a senior at Castlebrook High School, and I don't have a girlfriend right now, 'cause the girls round here be trippin', and my mom said I don't have time for no girls right now anyway."

"Is that right," said Mattie, humorously.

She walked to her beautifully made bed and grabbed the beautiful handmade quilt that lay flawlessly across the bottom. She walked over sat calmly for a moment and covered her legs with the quilt.

Deuce sat dazed and confused, waiting for Mattie, whose attention had gone to the tea kettle that had begun to whistle.

"All right now, let's have some tea," she said, nodding, grabbing the teapot with her apron. "Now, where do we begin? I know, tell me about your family."

"Well it's a long story, Miss Mattie," he responded solemnly, slouching.

"I got time, child."

"Well when I was about five, my dad was sent to prison for something he didn't do, and then it messed up my whole family. Then my grandmother died and we were real close, and everything got crazy," his voice cracking. "But I made a promise to my grandmother that I would not get in trouble and stay in school 'cause I want to be a lawyer and get my pop out of prison."

"That is a lot for such a young man as yourself."

"Yeah, but my mom is strong and she's back in school and one day things are gonna get better. I get good grades and I have lots of offers from colleges, but I pretend that I don't know nothing because my friends give me a hard time and it's just not good to be smart when you live in the 'hood.'"

"My goodness child, that must be a lot to carry on your shoulders? But yes, I believe things will get better for you."

"I remember my life was hard down South as well, we worked hard in the fields, but my folks always told us to work hard and one day times will change. We had so much love in my family--that makes a difference. We had to deal with the separation of negros and the whites, but one day I think we will all be together on good terms like me and my best friend Pamela."

"She was white Miss Mattie?" His eyebrows rose.

"Oh yes, we grew up together on the same property. Her parents sold property to my daddy, but didn't tell the other white folks 'cause it wasn't a good thing. They just thought we sharecropped."

"Wow that's a lot to deal with. I don't think I could have lived back there, that's too much."

"Yeah child, you had to be right quiet."

Deuce began admiring the colors on her wall as he started listening carefully to heartfelt stories of Mattie's life. When he crossed to the window to pull back the curtain the sun was just breaking ground over the horizon.

"Oh my God, the sun is coming up!" Deuce yelled.

He and Mattie had talked all night long.

Up quickly and reaching for the door, he exclaimed, "My mom is gonna kill me! What am I gonna to tell her?" he frantically beseeched at Mattie who sat peacefully sipping her tea.

"All is well, child. You run on home now, you'll see," she said with assurance and confidence.

"Thanks, Miss Mattie," he spoke in a guttural whisper, "I'll see you later."

"Yes indeed, child."

Closing the door, he felt a soft breeze that came and whirled around him as he ran up the stairs to his apartment. He turned the knob and held his breath in anticipation of her standing there, but much to his surprise the house was quiet and still. He crept by her room; she was still asleep. At that moment he heard Mattie's voice: "I told you all would be well."

Closing the door to his bedroom, he plopped down on the bed and cradled his head back onto his folded arms. Staring up at the ceiling, he thought about his evening with Miss Mattie, and what a gift he was confident she had become.

A short time later the excited voice of Angel startled him out of his rest.

"Deuce, get up and come here! Hurry!" she shouted from the kitchen.

"Ma! Don't do that! Man, you scared me! What's up?"

"Look," she said, pointing out the window.

Police cars were everywhere.

"Well, apparently some of your friends got into some trouble last night, 'cause the police have them sittin' on the curb, handcuffed," she said, looking suspiciously at Deuce.

"I told them not to go with Two-Strikes.

Aw man."

"What? What were they doing with him?"

Suddenly a pounding on the door made his stomach twist in sickening fear. Reluctantly opening the door, he was met by Linda, Rashad's sister, both panicked and crying.

"They're taking my brother to jail, Deuce!" she exclaimed.

Time seemed to stand still.

"I can't believe this Deuce! I would have never thought your friends would be sittin' on the curb like this! This is crazy," said Angel.

Without further delay Deuce ran outside. He paused, inhaled deeply and watched his best friends being placed into one of the police cars.

There was a large amount of noise; conversations were taking place all around him. He glanced over at Mattie, who was sweeping her stoop unaffected by everything going on around her. He just watched her. Who was this old lady? If she had not come along right on time, I would be in the back of one of the police cars too, he speculated.

Mattie stopped sweeping and paused momentarily, looking around as if surveying something. Finally, she glanced over at Deuce, never saying a word nor acknowledging him. She just stared.

Not sure of what to do, he nodded. Mattie smiled and motioned for him to come.

"Hello, how are you this morning?" she stated pleasantly brushing the dust from her apron and clearing her throat.

Deuce smirked, his head slightly tilted. "Good morning Miss Mattie. Man, this is a messed up day. I guess you saw my friends get arrested a few minutes ago?"

"Everyday is a good day. It just depends on how you look at it," she stated simply. "Every man chooses his destiny, Deuce. Which path will you choose, because time waits for no man?"

Huh? What is she talking about, time waitin' for no man, what's that? He thought.

"I don't know Miss Mattie; I guess I don't get it. We gotta make money somehow, either legally or illegally, and in the 'hood we choose the illegal way 'cause it's fast money."

"Is that all you think about your life Marcus Freeman, Jr.?"

"Not really. I think about bein' a lawyer and I really want to help my dad and I don't want to disappoint my mom or my grandmother's memory, but I understand why my friends did it."

"You reckon you'll choose different next time if'n you are asked?"

"It depends on whether I need the money and what is happening with my friends."

"Where I'm from, the old folks would say that if'n you lay with the dogs you'll get up with fleas. You understand what that means, child?"

"Yeah, I understand but it's not that easy." His hands flicked nervously down the front of his shirt.

"You are a very intelligent young man with a good heart, and in time you'll see just what you have to offer. And that it reaches far beyond these city limits that you have built a wall around."

Mattie began sweeping again, ignoring Deuce momentarily.

"I reckon all the excitement's done for the day, so you best be getting' to school, huh?"

"I guess you're right, I'll see you later maybe?" He lifted his shoulders briefly.

"I'm thinkin' that would be a good thing."

"Hey Miss Mattie, how was your day?" Deuce walked over with a hop in his step. "It was good. Got lots of things to do and folks to help so I am right busy."

"Folks to help? Whatcha mean?"

"Oh, one day you'll understand but we got to help you right now, so come on in." She walked over to the two-burner stove and turned on the fire under the kettle.

Deuce entered quickly and grabbed two teacups from the rickety cabinet, walked over and plopped down in the chair at the table, which made its normal squeaking. He brushed the wrinkles from the lace placemat atop the tablecloth.

"How's things goin' for you? With school almost done I reckon you'll be headin' off to college."

The teakettle whistled and Mattie motioned for Deuce to get up and pour the water into the cups.

"It will be a hard decision, Miss Mattie." said Deuce, placing the kettle back on the burner and sitting down. "Do I want to go far away from you and my Mom, or stay close by so I can help out?"

"Oh no, child, you got to go where you get the best education, and make new friends. Don't worry yourself about me. I'll be just fine, and besides I'll be leavin' soon." Mattie smoothed the wrinkles out of the quilt over her knees as she slowly rocked in the chair staring blankly at Deuce.

"Leavin'! Where you goin', Miss Mattie?"

He scooted toward the edge of his chair, leaning on every word like a child taking his first step.

"Oh child, don't you fret none, you just work on gettin' into school, and we'll take care of the rest later."

There was an uneasy silence at the table. Mattie rose up slowly and walked to the window while Deuce watched her, fascinated.

"I was hoping you could help me with my speech," his voice quivering.

"Looky here, your Mama's coming' down the street and her arms are full of bags. Best you need to get on out there and help her."

Deuce walked quickly to the window. Deuce pulled back the drape, confusion clouding his face.

"My mom never gets home this early. I hope everything is okay. Guess I better go help." He cleared his throat, and tapped lightly on the window seal.

"Yes indeed, and I guess I'll see you later so we can work on that graduation speech of yours."

"Yeah, okay, Mattie, we'll see." Suddenly his stomach tightened and his mouth became dry and sticky. "Mattie, can I ask you something?"

Observing the expression on his face, she answered quickly, "Oh, not now child, your Mom needs help so go on and we'll talk later." She began to hum in a whisper that was barely audible.

Deuce looked over at her in surprise. "All right, no problem. I'll just come back later."

He opened the door slowly making the squeaking more apparent.

"Hey Ma, what are you doin' home so early?" He grabbed a couple of the bags from a smiling Angel, and kissed her lightly on the cheek.

"We finished early and I had a few extra dollars so I decided to stop by the store and get some of your favorite things and come home and hang out with my son,"

she said, smacking him on the butt.

"Aw, I hate when you do that." He turned and stood stationary.

"Okay, but you're gonna miss that when you leave for school."

"I know, don't remind me."

"Hey what's wrong? How's Miss Mattie? I saw you come out of her spot?"

"She's cool." he said, walking up the stairs and reaching back to Angel for the keys to open the door. "But she said something kinda strange."

"What?"

"That she may be leavin' soon, then when I tried to ask her about it you showed up and she made me leave to help you."

They walked in and placed the bags on the table, spilling a glass of water that he had forgotten to put in the sink when he left for school.

"Oh man, really Deuce, she said that?" Angel snatched a towel and dabbed the water up. "And I'm not going to say anything about this glass you left on the table!"

"I know, I know, sorry," he said, grabbing another towel and wiping the floor. "I hope she doesn't leave anytime soon. I just have my speech to take care of first then I'll worry about Miss Mattie."

"Well, time will tell. Now let's get this food ready."

Late that night, Deuce was overwhelmed with the thoughts of graduating, and leaving for college, but more than that, Mattie leaving.

A short time later he heard the faint sound of Mattie singing. Deuce crept down the stairs. She was smiling pleasantly as always, humming to herself.

"Well hello there, Marcus Freeman, Jr. Are you ready for your big day?"

"I think so," he answered quickly.

"Well, I guess we can go inside and sit for a minute." She leaned the broom against the side and opened the door, causing Deuce to be overcome with the aroma of lavender. He also fixed his eyes on a tall vase filled with sunflowers which was posed gallantly in the corner of the room. The smell was intoxicating.

"I love that smell!" he cried, throwing his jacket on the small stool that sat nearest the door. He continued to inhale and exhale deeply, enjoying every breath of the lavender he could consume.

Mattie turned on the burner under the teapot, while Deuce did his usual of grabbing two teacups and place-mats and placing them neatly on the table, removing any wrinkles that had formed.

Deuce took his seat smiling unambiguously.

He looked up, taking another deep breath.

"Miss Mattie, I never believed in like spiritual stuff, but my grandmother did and she said promised me that I would be protected. I used to hear her prayin' at night but I was never sure until I met you. There is somethin' about you, Mattie Fitch, but I can't put my finger on it--but it's different."

Mattie chuckled.

"You keep on believin', child, and trust that inner voice. It will never steer you wrong."

"Mattie, tell me some more about your family."

Mattie became trance-like as she began talking about her childhood in Darlington, smiling to herself as if she was back there.

"It's a beautiful place, Deuce. If you ever get a chance you must go there and visit," chuckling softly.

"How old were you when you came to California, Miss Mattie?" He leaned in as if he was going to hear a secret.

"I don't right remember, but I travel around a lot here and there doing jobs for people."

"Yeah, but how old were you when you left home?" The teacup rattled loudly as he placed it on the saucer, startling both of them.

Mattie picked up her cup and took a sip. Cleared her throat eyebrows raised. "So what time did you say the graduation was?"

Deuce sat quietly wringing his hands. "Mattie, are you ignoring me?"

"Oh goodness no, child, I was just gettin' ready to say that." Suddenly the alarm clock began to ring, startling both of them.

"Oh, time for my appointment," she said hurriedly. "I've got to go!"

"You gotta go?" he asked curiously. "I didn't know."

"Time just flies, you know," Mattie said, excitedly. "I've got to get to my appointment."

Opening the door she looked over at Deuce smiling slyly. "I will see you later."

Deuce looked confused and agitated. "I'm done anyway, so I'll see you later?"

"Don't worry; things will work out. You head on home now."

Deuce, bewildered, gathered his jacket and walked to the door, Mattie in tow.

He walked up the stairs slowly, stopping for a moment and listening to the recognizable sounds of the children that were running, playing and laughing. They made him smile.

Suddenly he felt a slight bit of fear. Am I ready? What if something happens to my mom while I'm away? What if I don't make it at school--what am I gonna do? He was overwhelmed.

Opening the door, he went inside.

"Hey Deuce, what's up, son? You ready?" Angel spoke enthusiastically.

"Yeah, just so much going on in my head," sitting down at the table exhaling loudly. "Ma, life is going to be good, just wait and see, especially when I get dad out of jail. I am going to work hard and make you proud; I just wish Grandma was here to see this day."

The room became completely silent.

"Me too," Angel stated quickly. "She is with us in our hearts, our memories, and she would want us to have a good time today. We have come a long way, Deuce; don't forget what could have happened."

"Well, it's almost that time so I better start getting ready."

Graduation Day

Graduation day finally arrived, and it would be better than Deuce had anticipated.

It seemed like a long time since he had seen his friends, but through the luck of the draw and some decent public defenders they were all able to get off with short time. Just in time for graduation.

He headed down to Mattie's place to get some last-minute words of wisdom.

He knocked hard.

"Good morning, Deuce," Mattie said eagerly. "Come on in. I just put the pot on 'cause I had a feelin' you was headed this way."

"Well it's my big day, and then I'll be headed off to college next." His voice held a tone of excitement. He pulled the chair away from the table and sat quickly.

"I am very proud of you, young man."

Deuce smiled, sipping his hot tea slowly.

"I just want you to know how much I appreciate you. You saved my life. And until we met, the only other person that really believed I could do anything, besides mom was my Grandmother. I love you, Miss Mattie," he whispered shyly. "You taught me so much about trusting and believing in myself. I could be sittin' in jail right now, but you showed up right on time, and so when I give my speech at graduation you better believe I'm gonna mention your name." he stated proudly.

"Oh Child, I am so very proud of you. You wanted a chance, your heart cried out for it, and I was sent to answer,"

Mattie spoke earnestly. "But you must always remember that it was your strength that got you to this point; I was just here to assist you in finding your way.

You made the choice not to get into the car that day, and instead assist an old woman who was in need. And for that you have received the ultimate gift: life," wiping her brow.

"I will make you proud, Miss Mattie. I am going to become the best civil rights attorney ever; first, I'll get my father out of jail, and then help others that have been treated unjustly. You watch and see."

"I reckon you will, Deuce. In fact I know'd you will. There are many folks that live with regrets, like your friends who should have never tried to make fast money, and now they have a mark on their record and almost missed one of the most important days of their lives. If they could do it over I am confident they wouldn't make the same choice. But it's up to you to be the one who makes a difference, and shows the ones who have supported, believed in and loved you that there are possibilities beyond this place you call the jungle."

Deuce looked up, took a deep breath, and smiled.

College Day

Deuce woke up early the next morning, reaching over and smacking his hand down on his alarm clock for the last time. Pulling back his curtain, he noticed the sky was strikingly blue, with two bundles of clouds hurdling together giving the appearance of a heart. He became entranced. There was a feeling of excitement in the air as he laid in bed thinking about what was before him. In just a few hours he would be taking that ride to college and beginning a new journey. No longer able to fight off the sweet smell of bacon frying he jumped up and headed to the kitchen.

"Good mornin', Ma," walking over and kissing her on the cheek.

"Hey you, how you feelin'this mornin'?"

"I'm cool. A little nervous," he answered, looking around.

"Sit down and eat somethin' before you leave your ma and head off to college."

"Aw Ma, come on now," and without waiting for a reply, he added, "come on, let's eat.

"I love you," Angel spoke softly, trying to fight back tears.

"I love you, too," he said emotionally, looking out of the window.

As they ate breakfast, they reminisced about old times and shared thoughts on how far they had come.

The time flew by. Deuce realized that he had not gotten to see Mattie.

"It's almost time to go, and I haven't seen Mattie."

He walked to the window, taking a half-glance over at Angel.

"I'm gonna go down and see if she's around."

"Okay son, but don't take to long now."

The telephone began to ring.

He opened the front door and headed straight down to Mattie's place. Turning the corner, he noticed a white envelope with a sunflower in the corner taped to the door. "Marcus Freeman, Jr." was written beautifully in the center.

Immediately he felt a knot in his stomach and was overcome with emotion, but couldn't touch the envelope.

After a couple of minutes, he exhaled and swallowed hard. Biting his lip, he reached up and took the envelope in his hand, catching a scent of lavender.

Carefully and gently he unsealed the back, his eyes beginning to fill with tears; he knew she was gone. Taking a seat on the stoop, he read the note:

My Dearest Marcus,

What a wonderful day this is. Being grateful for all that has come to you is critical and you must always remember where you could have ended up.

One other thing—it is important to remember that you have a great work you have to do. Stay focused on what you are trying to accomplish. There will be no excuse for failure.

I am needed elsewhere, but I will return when the time is right. Read these words often, and speak your intention.

You have opened doors where once stood walls. Walk through and embrace the newness that awaits you. Believe in this process, trust it. You will not fail. Be honest—it creates a road of credibility and ethical standing. Always do your best, no more, no less.

You will graduate from college and go to law school. Ask for what you want, look for it in the small places and you will find it I believe in you.

On June 11, 2013 at 12 noon meet me in the JL Square by the pier; I will have something for you. Until then.

"Your dreams are your reality asleep, wake them up."

Best regards,

Mattie Fitch

He fought back the tears, got to his feet, and proceeded back upstairs. I will amount to something, and make my family proud, he thought. Let the journey begin he whispered to himself.

Chapter 5
White Boys Can Jump

"AHHH BOOM!!!!" The young men in the crowd yelled in unison as they anticipated the next moment, watching, waiting in eager anticipation of his often-failed attempts. The sounds of laughter engulfed the basketball court where the neighborhood guys gathered daily to either play ball or pick up the young women who watched with longing and high hopes. There was a wide variety of men with a vast array of skills, but all of them had one attitude in common—either play ball or go home.

They were serious about basketball, many of them believing that it was their ticket out of the 'hood, as it had been for some of their predecessors. Chris was confident in his ability, yet he was the only one in his crew that had failed the ultimate achievement: the dunk.

With so many missed opportunities, the ridicule had become too much. Now determination was his main focus.

He had spent many long hours studying, watching and emulating the skills of the very best, and he was sure today would be the day. It was vitally important to have the ability to showcase your skills in the neighborhood, especially when you were one of the only white boys living there.

His mother decided that the easiest way to acclimate Chris to his new life and surroundings was to place him in sports. From the moment he took a basketball in his hands, he excelled in the game. He was a natural, and despite his height, he gained immediate success and acceptance. He was always on the court practicing, trying to improve anyway he could.

Chris T. Mills was known in the triangle as *Boom* because of the sound that resonated from the rim of the old, broken-down basketball hoop every time he tried, then missed, his slam dunk.

At 5'8", he was determined not to allow his height to be a factor. After all, many of his idols in the NBA were small in stature yet great in accomplishments.

There was something mysterious about Chris. His head was kept clean-shaven so that he could camouflage his being completely white. He had beautiful hazel eyes that seemed to look through you, and nice round lips that he often licked as he cocked his head to the side before shooting the basketball. His slightly bowed legs made him irresistible to many of the girls. But Chris had a secret.

"Told you white boys can't jump, Boom. Get outta there, boy," one of the fellas yelled, as a rash of teasing and laughter from the guys standing around followed. He had again missed his dunk again.

"Whatever, man!" he mumbled, grabbing the ball again and turning towards the net. "What you gon' say when I'm hittin' them three-pointers in the NBA, boy?" He spoke arrogantly, trying not to appear embarrassed from his previous miss. He turned, throwing up a three point shot from the corner. It entered the net.

"Swoosh!" he yelled, running to the sideline and quickly sitting down.

Laughter erupted.

Basketball was Chris's life. He could be found on the court for three to four hours a day, trying to improve his game, all the while imagining that he played for the NBA. Losing focus was not an option.

Chris did not have a choice with his life—he had to work extra hard to be accepted, as growing up in the 'hood surrounded by African Americans and Hispanics was no easy task.

He lived with his mom Tina, his sister Sydnee, and his step-father Maurice. Tina is a white woman and a single parent who, when Chris was three, "defected" from the suburbs (as she called it) to move where she felt she belonged. Tina and Chris's father divorced when he was around one year old, leaving her to raise him alone. When Chris was four, Tina met Maurice who drove a bus for the transit company. They married about one year later.

Having a biracial sister helped Chris "pass" in the neighborhood because, even when asked, he could deny being completely white. After many years he had become just one of the boys, and not even those closest to him knew the truth.

Chris had the responsibility of taking care of his younger sister while their parents worked. Sydnee was determined to get into trouble, no matter the costs to Chris. As the game ended he checked the time; it was nearly five o'clock, so he headed home.

Opening the door, he was met by Sydnee who had been trying desperately to get out of the house before he got home.

"Where you goin', Syd?" Chris asked sternly.

"Outside for a minute," she snapped rudely.

"Nope, you ain't goin' nowhere. Tomorrow is the first day of school and it's getting' late. I'm not goin' to hear Ma's mouth 'cause of you!"

Chris leaned his back against the door, with folded arms smirking widely.

"Move back," he stated sarcastically, flicking his fingers.

"Whatever! You ain't my daddy," She said, rolling her eyes as she again reached for the door. "Move, punk!" she yelled.

Chris looked at her unsympathetically.

"I'm serious, Syd. I'm not getting' in trouble for you no more. I said no!"

They stood in a standoff. Sydnee, finally giving in, turned and walked over to the sofa, plopping down so hard she sent the pillows flying, clearly planning her get away.

Chris headed for the kitchen to look for something to eat. Suddenly the front door opened.

"Hey bring your behind back here!"

He just barely caught a glimpse of her as she ran out of the door down the stairs, out of sight.

Chris headed out behind her, clearing the stairs two-by-two. Rounding the corner at the bottom he nearly tripped over a young girl sitting quietly reading a book on the stoop.

"Whoa, what are you doing right there?" He said, clearly surprised. "I could have hurt you or me."

"I'm reading." She replied, never looking up from her book. "Why aren't you paying attention?"

Chris, somewhat taken aback, stopped and looked curiously at this interesting young girl. Exhaling deeply he turned and scanned the street.

He sat down on the steps examining the girl who was clearly not fazed by all the commotion taking place around her.

"Excuse me, I was wondering if you saw a girl run by just a minute ago, and if so which way did she go?" he asked inquisitively.

"Maybe, it depends," she responded indifferently, still not looking up from her book.

"Depends on what?" he said smiling, bending down in front of her, trying to make eye contact.

"On why you looking for her, that's what," she responded firmly, finally looking over the top of the book.

"What is up with you? Can't you just answer a question?" He said, laughing to himself.

"Yes, I can." She closed the book.

"My name is Mattie Lee Fitch," smiling grandly. "And yours?"

Chris laughed out loud.

"My name is Christopher T. Mills, but my friends and family sometimes call me Boom."

"And I'm Sydnee Michelle Nicole Denise Kristal Marie Brown, but you can call me Baby Doll," she laughed, jumping out from behind the building.

"Baby Doll, why they call you that and what does the T stand for?" Mattie responded, confused but not fazed by their behavior.

"'cause I'm the baby, I'm a doll, and why you talk so funny?" Sydnee responded boastfully, rolling her head and smacking her lips.

"Sometimes I crack myself up!" Sydnee said, pacing between the two of them.

"No, she is a pain in the butt is what she is. Don't pay her any attention, Mattie," he stated roughly. "Do you live in this building, 'cause I've never seen you around here before, and where are you from?" looking slightly puzzled.

"I am from Darlington, South Carolina, and I live right over there with my grandmother and aunt," she said, pointing to a door nestled underneath the stairs.

"Darlington, South Carolina! Never heard of it and girl you better stop lying. Isn't that the storage room?" Sydnee stated arrogantly.

Chris glanced coldly at Sydnee, who was staring blankly in disbelief.

Mattie sat quietly considering what to do.

"No, it is not a storage room, thank you very much."

She scooted toward the edge of the stoop. "And I would never tell a lie because it's wrong," she answered confidently. "Besides it has more than enough room. We are quite happy there, and it's just temporary."

They all stopped for a moment looking toward the sound of sirens headed in their direction. In no time at all three police cars came to an abrupt stop across the street, taking a few young men out of a black Mercedes Benz and having them sit shamefaced on the curb.

"I can't wait to get up outta this madness," he said kicking the bottom step. "This has gotten way old."

Sydnee took a seat next to Mattie on the stairs.

"You like to read, huh?" she asked nosily pushing up the book exposing the cover.

"Of course, don't everyone?" Mattie answered inquiringly.

"I hate reading, it's boring and I ain't got time," snapped Chris.

"I'm just pretendin' I love to read," she replied, quietly annoyed.

They all stopped and stared at the chaos taking place with the police across the street, the sun setting moment by moment.

"How old are you, Mattie?" Sydnee asked, standing to her feet. "And don't pay him no attention. He's just mad 'cause he can't read!" she said, pointing her finger in his Chris's face and laughing loudly.

"Yeah whatever, girl," slapping her finger down. "I can read better than you can!" he responded, clearly frustrated.

"Yes, of course you can," Mattie stated compassionately. "I am twelve years old, and I'm reading Paul Laurence Dunbar. He is one of our history's greatest

African American poets, you know," staring curiously at them both.

He turned to face her. "Who!?" he laughed. "I've never heard of him."

"Well, it seems someone has a lot to learn. Have you ever read poetry?" Mattie asked, closing the book and looking directly into his eyes. "Reading poetry opens the windows of your mind," she said excitedly.

Sydnee rolled her eyes. "This is too much for me. I'll be right back!"

"Come right back, Syd, for real!" Chris yelled firmly.

"Sorry about that, but naw, I ain't got time for reading. I'm getting' ready for the NBA, girl, that's my dream," he said, raising his hands as if he was shooting a basketball. "You better ask somebody!" he stated boldly.

"Well, who do you suggest I ask?" she asked, looking oddly at Boom. "Why don't you make time to read?"

He stopped and sat down.

"You're different, Mattie Fitch. I like you, but unfortunately I don't have time to sit and talk anymore. We gotta get in before my moms gets home." He attempted to stand.

"Wait a minute, I want you to hear something," she said, tugging slightly on his sleeve.

"Okay, but for just minute," He looked down at the time on his cell phone. "I got a minute."

He sat quietly, listening intently, as she read.

He had his dream, and all through life, worked up to it through toil and strife. Afloat fore'er before his eyes, it colored for him all his skies.

The storm-cloud dark, above his bark, the calm and listless vault of blue, took on its hopeful hue, it tinctured every passing beam. He had his dream. He labored hard and failed at last, his sails too weak to bear the blast. The raging tempests tore away, and sent his beating bark astray. But what cared he for wind or sea!

He said, "The tempest will be short, my bark will come to port." He saw through every cloud a gleam. He had a dream.

Dunbar, Paul Laurence, "He had His Dream."

"It sounds a lot like you, don't you think, Chris T. Mills?" Mattie spoke quietly. "Almost reads real."

Closing the book, she stared innocently at Chris who didn't speak for a moment. He just stared.

Mattie continued to stare at him strangely, while he smiled nervously. "Are you all right, Chris?"

"Um, yeah I'm cool. Thanks, Mattie. I really enjoyed talking with you." he said, digging in his pocket for his cell phone."

"Oh my god, it's six o'clock," he said, looking around for Sydnee. "Man, the time has flown, but we gotta get." He motioned for Sydnee to come. "We gotta get in 'cause my moms be trippin' if we not in on time," he said, looking down again at his phone. "I'll talk to you later and you can finish telling me all about Mr. Dunbar, the famous poet," he said, laughing nervously.

"It was fun for me too. We can read it together next time, okay?" she said, looking at him oddly.

"Um sure, no problem," he replied, dismissing her. "Come on Syd, its late! Mattie, you don't wanna be sittin' out here by yourself. It can be dangerous!"

"I reckon you're right." Mattie got up and headed for her door. "I can't wait to read poetry together, Chris," she said, smiling widely.

"See ya later, Mattie Fitch!" Sydnee yelled, running by, taking the stairs two-by-two and disappearing out of sight.

Mattie opened her door, and looked back towards Chris.

"Is everything okay, Mattie?" he asked, waiting for her to go inside.

"Yes indeed, everything is fine," she said happily, her eyes twinkling. Opening the door slowly she entered quietly. "Good night and I'll see ya tomorrow."

Chris tiptoed over and leaned his ear against the door, listening. There was nothing but silence.

He paused, and looked around the neighborhood.

"Boom you better get up here, fathead!" Sydnee shouted from the top of the stairs.

"I'm comin', girl. Shut up!"

Summer had come to an end.

Chris got up early the next morning. Standing in the closet he scanned back and forth, trying to put together just the right outfit. He stopped and stared out of the window in anticipation of the beginning of his senior year.

Chris went into the kitchen. Everyone was already eating.

"Come on, boy. Sit down, now, you gonna be late on your first day as a senior!" said Tina, grabbing a hold of Chris's arm. "My baby is graduatin' and gettin' a full scholarship, then off to the NBA!" she stated proudly.

"Girl, give the boy a break. You know this is gonna be a rough year, but you can do this, Boom. You know that, right?" said Maurice, giving him a pound.

"I know, I am just so proud of my kids," she replied innocently. "Oh Chris, the paperwork came from UCLA, and I need you to read over it so we can talk about it this evening, okay?" Tina stated quickly.

"Um yeah, but I got practice tonight, so I'll be late," Chris said, stumbling over his words.

"Yeah," asked Tina, stopping at the door and looking back. "What's wrong with you?"

"Nothin'. I'm cool." He stood quickly, leaving his half-empty plate. "Come on Syd, let's bounce."

"Wait a minute," Sydnee responded loudly, glaring at Chris. "I'm almost finished!"

"All right you two, that's enough." Tina replied without looking back. "See you later, and come straight home, Sydnee."

"Bye!" yelled Sydnee from the kitchen table.

"Come on girl!" said Chris, as he walked over and opened the door.

"Shut up, boy. You can't rush perfection," said Sydnee, who stood up and sauntered past Chris.

"Perfection, perfection—girl, please." Looking out into the hallway. "You can't even spell perfection, come on."

At the bottom of the stairs sat Mattie, reading a different book. Chris stopped for a moment to say hello. Sydnee waved and kept going, catching up to a group of her friends.

"Well good mornin', Chris T. Mills. How you?" Mattie asked cheerfully.

"I'm good. Hey, call me Boom. All my other friends do."

"All right then, I reckon I will," she said nodding her head. "You off to school this mornin', huh?" she asked.

"Yep, it's my first day, and it's a big one." He put his backpack down and looked at his cell phone. "I got lots of stuff I need to happen, Mattie, so keep your fingers crossed."

"Don't you worry one bit. If you believe in somethin' hard enough, it'll be yours, you just wait and see," she stated agreeably.

"Thanks, Mattie," he said, smiling. "Hey, come on. I'll walk you to school," he said, glancing around.

"Oh, no I go to school at home, so I'll see ya when you come in. We got a lot of work to do," she said, standing up and walking to her door.

"Okay," looking confused. "Oh, I got basketball practice, so I'll see you after that though."

Chris turned, waved goodbye and joined a group of kids who were walking to school.

It was a long walk home from basketball practice that day. Chris was just looking around when he noticed Mattie in the distance sitting on the stairs reading a book.

This girl is always reading, he thought, approaching slowly. He stopped bouncing the ball, and stared in admiration. Could she be the answer he was looking for?

Filled with excitement, he started to jog.

Approaching, he noticed several books stacked neatly next to her.

"Hey Mattie Fitch, what's up?" he said eagerly.

Mattie was staring into her book, her big brown eyes transfixed, almost magical.

"Oh, not too much I reckon, just readin' my book," she answered, looking up with a twinkle in her eye.

"Mattie, I got a question for you," Chris asked nervously, biting the inside of his lip. "What you really think about reading?"

"I'm mighty glad you asked," she said, closing the book. "Please forgive me for sayin' so, but I haven't seen much reading' goin' on 'round here. Folks don't spend much time readin', and if you don't know how to read, how do you expect good things gon' come your way? You just can't be who you was meant to be without it."

Mattie looked directly at Chris, but neither one of them spoke.

A few minutes passed.

Suddenly, pulling the book closer to her body, she repeated, in a corrective tone, "You can't be who you're supposed to be without it, you know, but why you askin'?"

He sat down beside her, and in a matter-of-fact manner, he responded.

"I don't know. I just figured that readin' didn't matter much, what's the point. But I'm not real sure about that anymore, pausing."

"The point is," Mattie interrupted, reopening her book, "you can go wherever and do whatever you want in here." She held the book up in the air, glancing over at Chris. "And most of all, become whoever you want to be."

Mattie looked over at Chris, who was visibly relieved.

"I am sometimes amazed at how folks can just take the most basic things for granted," she said disapprovingly.

"What do you mean?" he asked.

"Things that are given to us at no cost like our minds, bodies, and spirits we have been taught to take for granted," she said sincerely. "And we believe things we buy—you know the stuff that we think says what we are worth and that can be taken from us by other folks, or destroyed in storms or sumthin' that we think is important. But it isn't who we really are."

Chris sat staring at her listening intently, nodding in agreement, while Mattie's big brown eyes sparkled in the afternoon sun.

"Is that the life you want to live, Chris?" Mattie said slowly, glancing over at him. "Who are you really? Are you proud of what you do?"

"Naw, are you kiddin'?" he responded suddenly. "That's why I play ball, so I can get outta here, get my family a better life. Nobody wants to live like this," he said, pointing his fingers at the apartment building. "The folks who live here have given up on life. There's nothin' to believe in. Well, let me take that back." He put the basketball down and walked over and sat down next to Mattie. "Some of them have, I won't say all. There are some families that have lived in this neighborhood for years, and they are good people, hard workin' folks like my parents. Then there's some who don't have a choice, and how can you believe in something that's never given you anything? The drug dealers drive around in big cars and flash lots of cash, so what do the youngsters do when they have that type of example?" He paused, scanning the area. "Most of the time your parents are in jail or on drugs, and unless you are good in sports, the opportunities just aren't there. 'cause if you want to know the truth, being smart just ain't cool. Everyone will think you are just tryin' to be better than the rest, and you don't want that. It's unnecessary drama."

Pausing for a moment, Mattie cleared her throat, and in a parental tone she said, "Learnin' to read is an obligation that you owe yourself. It is a choice. And without it, the consequences can and will be a life that lacks the basic necessities. I'm not sayin' it's easy for everyone, but the same effort that you put into the success of basketball you should put in your wantin' to learn. What would you like me to do?" she asked, picking up two books and placing them on her lap.

Chris hesitated, sitting for a second, trying to gather his thoughts.

"This is really hard for me, but there are two things that I've never told anyone before, not even my folks know. One reason is because I played basketball so well that none of my friends ever questioned it. And the other is that all of my teachers would just pass me knowing full well I shouldn't have." His voice shaking, he cleared his throat. "Well, um," he said, stammering nervously.

"You can tell me anything, Chris. I've always been good wit' secrets," Mattie interjected genuinely.

"Well," he said, starting to fidget. "I can't read."

Mattie sat quietly staring blankly into his eyes while he gathered himself.

"Well, I can read a little bit, but not like I should. And I gotta pass this test so I can get my scholarship. My dreams depend on it," he said, wringing his hands and cracking his knuckles loudly. "And one more thing that's just as hard to talk about." He turned his back towards her muttering to himself.

"Well what is it, I can't hear you?" Mattie interrupted.

"All right, all right. I'm not really black, Mattie. I just wanted to be accepted and I've been pretendin' so long that if I say somethin' now, I don't know what people will say."

Chris stood, his heart pounding, staring at Mattie who didn't seem surprised. He walked a few steps away, turned around and walked back and sat down on the stairs next to Mattie.

She blinked several times and continued to stare at Chris.

"I will help you with your readin', and you gonna find it's easier than you think. Learnin' to read is simple, and you have it in you," she said happily. "My job is just to help you practice the art of readin'. It's like playing basketball. But the way you feel about yourself or trustin' the people who are around you, well, that's somethin' else all together."

Chris sighed.

"I know, but I figured what difference it made. My sister is biracial and my pops is black, and besides no one's ever asked me. They just assumed I was mixed, too."

"Or maybe they know and just aren't sure why you don't tell the truth," she said, pausing briefly. "You've got to be true to yourself; otherwise no one will ever trust you."

Mattie nodded.

"Can we talk about that later? I really need to get help with my readin'."

"Well let's get started because we're not going to get anywhere just sittin' here."

Mattie reached in a worn bag and pulled out a book, a small tablet, paper and a pen.

Chris looked puzzled.

"Okay, one of the first things you want to do when you're reading is to write down any words that you don't know and then you can look them up later. Then you'll know what they means," she said studiously, flipping the pages of the tablet.

Chris sat staring blankly.

"There may be a lot of words that I won't know." He sniffed and look around. "I'm already gettin' frustrated. It's gonna be tough," he groaned.

"You know, Chris," she responded patiently, "you can't give up. You're right, it may be tough in the beginning, but it's gonna be worth it at the end. Did you know how to shoot the ball right away, or did you have to practice?"

"I practiced a lot," he replied.

"Well then, you have to look at this like basketball practice. I know for sure that when you're finished you'll be happy with the outcome."

"Are you really twelve, Mattie?" he asked inquisitively, as he flipped through the pages of one of the books. "I can't figure you out. You don't act like you're twelve, that's for sure. You got lots of wisdom and you're really smart for a kid, that's for sure."

Mattie smiled, staring blankly at Chris but never responding to the statement. She began shuffling through some papers lying in her lap then after a few curious exchanges, she came to an abrupt stop.

"All right…here we are, let's get started," Mattie said with poise. With care she handed Chris another book with the words *I Can Read* engraved perfectly on the front. "Now this book is very special, she said, rubbing on the face of the book. "I learned to read by usin' it, and you will too," smiling widely.

The book was bound beautifully by an aged leather cover that oozed timelessness. Opening it carefully, he glanced naively over at Mattie. The pages were crinkled old and worn, but soft and supple. He was in awe. Something magical started happening.

Mattie rose suddenly. "Okay, Chris, We gon' meet everyday for one hour after practice, rain or shine, right here on these steps. I need to go right now, but we'll begin tomorrow."

Chris followed her toward her door, trying to get in one final word.

"Where you goin', Mat?" he asked curiously.

"I have to go in for a bit. Gotta take care of some things, but I'll see ya later!"

"Oh okay, Bye." The door closed in his face. "I'll see you tomorrow!" he yelled through the door.

Chris stood looking puzzled for a moment. He shook his head, picked up his ball and scooted up the stairs.

After several weeks Chris had taken his reading skills to a new level. The enthusiasm that emerged from him coupled with the energy that radiated around him was contagious.

"Mattie, you are like a drill sergeant with the reading," he said, laughing hysterically. "But I know one thing for sure is I wouldn't be on this level if it wasn't for you."

Chris picked up the book bag and reached inside and grabbed the tablet. "There are hardly no words left that I don't know—look Mat," he said, pointing to the list that had three words left. "I knew I could do this and the funny thing is it took a twelve-year-old kid to help me. Boy, if my sister and friends knew I would never hear the end of it, that's fo' sho'."

"I really didn't do anything special, you did it all and when you get that scholarship it will prove just how practice pays off."

Chris glanced down at his cell phone and checked the time. "Man, we are having a special practice today, and I gotta get, but I'll talk to ya later," he said, handing her the tablet.

"Well, I'll be here," Mattie said, thumbing through the book.

"All right then, bye."

"Bye now."

Today's basketball practice would be uncommon. A couple of scouts were coming to check out the team, and Chris knew he needed to come ready to showcase his skills, possibly for the last time. Entering the gym, the energy was high. The guys were scrambling around chasing balls, grabbing balls and shooting as many shots as possible, trying to make a good impression. Chris was anxious, but not willing to take any unnecessary chances.

It was important to demonstrate his leadership abilities as well.

Something strange was in the air. He felt an itch of nervousness as he approached the bench where some of his teammates were huddled around.

One of the players looked up. "What's up, Boom! You betta get out there, boy, and do your thang." They greeted each other with an enthusiastic handshake.

"Yes indeed, that's just what I'm gettin' ready to do! Come on, right here, everybody!" Chris responded confidently, running to the center of the floor.

The team ran to the middle of the court rallying around each other.

"All right, this is the chance for us seniors to do this, and we need the support of the rest of you to help us get it done," Chris said seriously, looking around the circle making eye contact with the teammates. "We can't do this without you, and it's now or never. We are a team, and we have to let them see how this championship team gets it done!

"Are you with me?" he yelled.

"YEAH!!!," they shouted in excitement.

"All right, Let's do this!"

The energy was beautiful: a mesmerizing display of skill and teamwork.

They ran through a few practice moves, running lines and layups. They were all looking impressive, especially Chris.

Coach stood watching intently, looking over the top of his bifocals and chewing a wad of bubblegum. He was a burly gentleman, with an itchy-looking moustache, a salt and pepper Afro that always looked uncombed. He wore his old Forty-Niners jersey with a matching baseball cap and a pair of worn-out Adidas.

Coach blew the whistle to end that round of practice and pulled his pants over his protruding stomach. "Five minutes!"

Chris ran over, sat on the bench and motioned for the guys to come over.

"All right y'all, we are on point, but you know we can always do better. You know these scouts know the game of basketball, and you ain't gonna make a good impression playin' raggedy ball," he said, both winded and assertive. "They know what they are looking for, and ball-hogs ain't it. You gotta show that you can be a team player, have whole-game attitude. Get your defense and offense game on point. There's no time for junk ball."

Coach interrupted. "You are absolutely right, Boom. I want you to understand a couple of things. These scouts came because they have heard about this number one team, and nothing else. First thing, they don't need you to say anything to them; talking is not what they are here to do. They wanna see some ball playin', straight offense and defense. Secondly, and most of all, they want to see some baskets made. Do I make myself clear?"

"Yeah Coach, but when they gon' let you know somethin', 'cause, man, I can't take this waitin' much longer," said Kai, a star player on the team.

"You gotta be patient, Kai. Just keep playin' team basketball; isn't that what I have taught you in the last four years?" Coach responded, looking down at his clipboard. "There is no such thing as 'me' basketball, 'cause it is not about you. But one thing I will tell is that there are a couple of you that don't need to worry. You're good to go. All right fellas," Coach clapped his hands together, huddling the team. "Oh yeah, I almost forgot." He stopped in his tracks and looked back at the team. "Don't forget the exit exam is coming up. Are there any of you who think you may have trouble passing? I need to know right now; we don't need any surprises!" Coach said, grimly looking over his glasses. "Okay, okay. Let's go!"

The team looked around at each other, but no one raised their hands. At that moment Chris remembered his meeting with Mattie after practice, but if anyone ever found out that a twelve-year-old girl was teaching him to read, that would be the end.

"All right, if everyone is good, then we should have no surprises. When it comes to making the final choices, we should be good to go. All right, get in here!" Coach pointed for the team to huddle together. "Okay, who's the best?" he yelled.

"The Vikes!" The team energetically replied.

"All right, let's do this!"

The team, full of enthusiasm ran back onto the court. Practice would be intense.

Coach blew the whistle, ending practice. Chris glanced up at the clock. It was 5:45. He had to meet Mattie in fifteen minutes. I'm gonna be late, he thought, grabbing his backpack.

"I think you all showcased your skills today and I am proud of you but each of you needs to be headed home, and get to studying for the test, right?" Coach stated sarcastically, motioning for Chris to come after releasing the rest of the players.

"What's up, Coach? I gotta get home. I have an something to do." Chris spoke quickly.

"That's what I was going to ask you, Mr. Mills," Coach stated curiously, staring at Chris. "Is everything all right, or is there something I need to know?"

"Naw, Coach, everything is cool," he said instantly. "It's actually better than you think."

"Okay, just remember this is an opportunity of a lifetime, and you can't let anything get in the way. I trust you; you are a great young man with a chance to do something great for not only yourself and your family, but this community." Coach placed his hand on Chris's shoulder looking him square in the eye. "You have to be true to yourself, son, and honesty is the one thing that can make or break you."

"I hear you. Coach," said Chris solemnly. He turned and headed towards the door, but he paused and looked back. "I know one of these days I'm gonna have to deal with my issues, Coach, but right now getting that scholarship and passing that test is my only focus, nothin' else."

"If you need me I'm here, you know that," he said walking toward the locker room. "Now get on home, and be here on time tomorrow—we got work to do."

Chris felt both physically and mentally exhausted on this walk home.

Rounding the corner, there was a bit of commotion down the street. The temptation to check it out was huge, but out of the corner of his eye he saw Mattie waiting patiently.

"Hey Mattie, what's up? Sorry I'm late. Coach called me in his office for a minute, but everything is cool."

"I see. Are you takin' good care of my book, Boom?" she asked inquisitively.

"Um, oh yeah don't worry about that, I got you, I won't let nothin' happen to that book," he replied nervously. "Why you always by yourself? Don't you get lonely?"

"I'm never lonely. There are always things to do and places to be. Our lives are very busy," she stated, straight-forward. "Besides, makin' sho' you pass this test is the main focus anyhow, right?"

"Well yeah, I was just wondering why you always by yourself, that's all," Chris said, sounding both anxious and embarrassed. "And you've never invited me in your house or nothin', that's all—it's cool."

"Well, you musta read my mind because it's a bit chilly this evening so I was gonna suggest we go on inside."

Mattie stood quickly and motioned for Chris to follow.

Chris looked surprised as he entered the house. A pleasant aroma filled his nostrils, and a warm, calming feeling engulfed his body.

"What's that smell?" he asked innocently.

"It's lavender, my favorite," she answered quickly.

She walked over to the cabinet and retrieved two glasses.

"You want somethin' to drink?"

"Yeah, sure."

He looked around, dropped his backpack by the door and took a seat at the table.

The room was very tidy; everything seemed to have a place. There were a few old photos logistically placed about the room. Two large vases filled with sunflowers sat boldly, one on the kitchen table and the other on a nightstand. They gave a sense of life to the room. Chris was mesmerized as he sat staring across the room at the photos.

"Boom…….Chris…..hello," Mattie spoke, in a soft whisper. "Are you ready to read?" she asked, handing him a glass of juice.

"Oh yeah, I'm sorry," said Chris, looking at the photos even closer. "Hey Mattie, tell me more about your childhood in South Caro…..lina, right?" he said, rubbing his hands together.

"Well, let me see" Mattie paused, got up from the table and walked over to the photos.

"I reckon this would take some time, but I, uh, will tell you a little. Then we got to get started 'cause its gonna be dark soon."

"No problem, I'm just curious" Chris said, placing his books and papers down on the table.

"All right."

Mattie got up and opened a drawer filled with little all types of oddities that he tried unsuccessfully to see. Reaching way in the back she pulled out an unusually shaped candle. After she lit it, its peculiar scent made Chris relax immediately.

Her voice seemed to transform, she became resolute, and he couldn't help but notice that his comfort level grew when she began speaking of her past. The more she talked, the harder it was to keep his eyes open.

"…and my granny's fried chicken was the best," she continued on.

He couldn't stay focused, but her voice was mesmerizing.

"…and then we would see our friends at the Giant tree, and uh……"

That was the last thing he remembered.

"Okay Boom, that's it for today," Mattie stated firmly.

Chris looked around bewildered.

"Mattie, did we read?" he stated, both confused and puzzled. "I feel like I went to sleep, but heard everything you said.

Mattie just smiled.

"I'll see you tomorrow, Chris," Mattie said enthusiastically, "But one thing I want you remember: you are a nice boy and people will like you for you. I find that if people spend their time trying to be what they think others will like, then they will never have time to find out who they really are. You have to believe in yourself enough to trust that who you are is enough."

"I never thought about it like that before, but it really shouldn't matter, should it? "Well goodnight Mattie, and thanks for everything. See you tomorrow."

"I'll see you tomorrow, and try to be on time."

She opened the door and gestured for him to go, closing the door after him as quickly as she had opened it.

Chris felt something strange deep down in the pit of his stomach, but he couldn't put his finger on it. He stood for a moment leaning his ear against the door. There was silence. He shrugged his shoulders, picked up the backpack and headed up the stairs, two by two.

Chris woke up around four o'clock in the morning and just lay in bed staring at the ceiling, his eyes blurry from lack of sleep. His nerves buzzed and burned.

Picking up the book Mattie had given him, he placed it on his chest and held on tight; it was comforting. In the back of his mind he could hear her voice. He got up, yawned loudly, stretched and walked over to his bedroom window. It was a beautiful May sunrise. Today was the day. The test and the championship game on Friday.

He continued to stare out of his bedroom window, contemplating his decision to wait until the final test day, but he wanted to make sure he had plenty of time to prepare. No time for errors.

Finally he walked over to his chair, picked up his perfectly pressed Levis, and Raider's t-shirt with matching baseball cap and got dressed in a hurry.

Chris went into the kitchen for breakfast but he wasn't really hungry. Everyone was already sitting around the table watching the usual morning news with no sound, blasting Rey on the morning radio show, and engaging in idle chitchat.

Sydnee was complaining about not wanting to eat what was made, and Tina and Maurice were ignoring her. Chris sat down by Sydnee, who gave him a dark and angry look, causing a round of laughter.

"This is test day, big man. You ready?" said Maurice proudly.

"I'm ready for this test. It's in the bag," Chris replied, downing a glass of orange juice.

"What time is the game on Friday?"

"Varsity plays at seven o'clock, man. It's big, Pop," Chris responded cautiously, reaching for the box of cereal.

"I am so proud of you. My baby is going to pass his test and get a scholarship all in one week, and then goin' to college just like his mama," Tina spoke joyfully.

"Um,whatever I'm the baby and he's a buster," Sydnee stated jokingly, exchanging hits with Chris.

"Seven, cool. I should be able to get there by second quarter, but remember hard, and watch your back," Maurice spoke excitedly. "I gotta get outta here and make that money. Come on baby, we gotta go."

"Okay Boom, you got this together. I know you can do it," Tina said lovingly, grabbing her purse and book bag. "I love you."

"I love you boy, and we are proud of you," said Maurice, heading for the door.

"Well, see you this evening, Boom. And Sydnee, come straight home," Tina said, her eyebrow rose.

"I will," Sydnee replied solemnly.

"You'll do fine on your test. I have a good feelin' about that," Tina smiled, closing the door.

"Thanks Ma," Chris bellowed through the closed door.

After about ten minutes there was a knock at the door. Deja, Sydnee's friend, had come by to walk to school with her.

"Hiiiiiiii, Boom," said Deja with a swooning tone.

"Yuck," said Sydnee sucking her teeth. "Come on girl, let's go."

Shutting the door, the girls disappeared out into the hallway and down the stairs.

Chris cleared the table and walked over to the mirror by the front door. He took one last look and repeated a couple of phrases written in the manual: *I Am a Genius, I Can Read.*

He turned around gathered his things and headed out the door.

At the bottom of the stairs Mattie stood, cheerful as ever. Nothing ever seems to bother *her*, he thought.

"Hey, Boom. Good mornin'," She spoke pleasantly, "Today is the big day, yes indeed."

"Yeah Mattie, it is," Chris stated anxiously. "I think I'm more nervous about the test than Friday's game. I know I'm prepared for the test."

"Be true to yourself, Chris. Folks ain't got time for nothin' else," she replied carefully. "You have done a lot to get where you are, now you need to be who you are, and everything else will work."

Chris stood there, staring at Mattie, listening intently.

Huh? He thought. What does she know?

"Thanks for everything Mattie, but I need to get to the school and get this test out of the way," he stated, looking concerned. "Oh yeah, you should plan to come to my game if you can."

"I'll see what I can do. Not sure if I can, but we'll see," she said quickly.

"All right, see ya later."

Chris headed down the sidewalk.

Suddenly, he turned, looked back and saw Mattie watching him. At that moment he heard her voice whisper, "Be true to you," as if she was standing right next to him talking. He shook it off and continued on his way.

Arriving at school, everyone was standing around waiting for the last bell to ring. He made his way to the cafeteria where the test would be administered.

Deep down Chris knew what Mattie meant, but why would that have anything to do with what he was trying to accomplish.

Be true to yourself—those are some strong words, he kept thinking. Was pretending to be African American wrong? I'm not hurting anybody. Or am I, he wondered.

Chris's stomach twisted. Even though he was prepared, he couldn't stop thinking about what Mattie had told him.

"Okay ladies and gentlemen, you have thirty minutes left," the test administrator said, loudly. "When you're finished, please bring all of your materials to me and leave quietly."

His face in his hands, he shook his head. It was over.

The Game

It had been a long week. Everyone had been waiting patiently for the results of the test but that was no longer Chris's focus; the championship game was here.

All the players arrived at the gym early, running through their plays and shaking off the nervousness. After about thirty minutes Coach called them into the locker room for their final pep talk.

"Okay fellas, this is it, no turnin' back now," Coach said enthusiastically. "I wanna see lots of defense, and remember to check in with Boom for signals, and be ready to feed off fast breaks!"

The energy in the locker room was growing more intense with every word that Coach spoke. It was now or never; they had to get it done.

He paused for a moment, making eye contact with all of the players.

"I also want to say to my seniors, this has been one hell of an experience, and I am so very proud to have had this opportunity to see you grow into some of the best basketball players in California!" he said both energetically and emotionally. "Many of you were awarded full scholarships and have been accepted to some of the best colleges in this country, and I am proud to have coached you."

The room became strangely quiet. The team stood in amazement for a moment. It was a rare for them to see this side of Coach.

"Come on, team captain, say something," said Coach quickly, shaking off his emotion and pointing to Chris.

Preoccupied, Chris didn't answer. The sound of Mattie's voice kept playing over and over in his mind: be true to yourself.

"Hey Boom! Wake up, fool. Coach is talkin' to you!" yelled Marcus, looking at him strangely.

"Say somethin' to the team. What's wrong with you?" Coach repeated.

"Um. Aw, man," Chris stuttered and stumbled over his words. "I got somethin' on my mind, and I need to tell you guys. Don't ask me why I waited until now, just I need to get this off my chest," he said, with a strange tone to his voice. "It's not that I didn't trust y'all, it's just I wasn't sure of how you would treat me."

"Get on wit it, punk. We ain't got all day! We got a championship to win!" yelled a couple of his teammates.

"What? You got some disease or somethin'?" said another player.

A burst of laughter sounded throughout the room.

Coach smiled slyly.

"Naw fool, shut up. All right man, gimme a minute." He took one final look around the room at his teammates who were waiting, curious. The sound of Mattie's voice whispered ran through his mind one last time.

"Okay, I'm not bi-racial, I mean I'm not African American, I'm really white," he said anxiously, his voice cracking and heart pounding.

He stood staring at his teammates who seemed rather uninterested.

"Is that it, punk? We knew that already!" shouted Kai, bursting into laughter.

"Yo' big mouth sister told everybody that long time ago, boy. You are the only one who didn't know. What took you so long to figure out who you were?" A roar of laughter and white-boy jokes immediately followed.

"You were raised right here wit' the rest of us, and you ain't never tried to be betta than nobody here," said Stefan confidently. "Yo' family's just tryin' to make it betta, so you cool wit' me, Brad Pitt!

Chris stood in front of his team, speechless.

"Okay fellas, let's get our focus back, especially now that we know Boom is white, we can get ready for this game," Coach said smiling at Chris. "Okay, are we ready?" Coach yelled loudly.

"YES!" shouted the entire team, jumping up out of their seats.

"Then let's do this!" Coach motioned for Chris to come over to where he was standing, high-fiving each player as they passed.

"So, how do you feel?"

"A whole lot better than I did before, how did you know?

"Boy I've known for years. I just wanna make sure that the young man who passed his exit exam knows who he is."

"For real coach, I passed! Oh man, you gotta be kiddin' me." Chris shouted enthusiastically. "I knew it!

"Whoever's been tutoring you worked a miracle. Now, with all that said let's go, sir. We have a championship to win!"

"She really did Coach, she really did," said Chris flashing back.

They shook hands and headed toward the entrance to the gym where the sounds of cheering and applause rang throughout. Cameras from local television stations were systematically stationed around the gym to catch every moment of this championship game.

The energy was high; each team had come to play.

The referee blew his whistle signaling the start of the game. As he tossed the ball in the air the players moved into position. Jay out-jumped his opponent and tapped the ball to Boom; the home crowd erupted in jubilation.

I gotta stay focused, can't get too excited, he thought, taking control and heading down the court.

The new plays were working; back and forth they drove down the court, shooting a steady stream of lay-ups and fade-aways. The scores were tallying up, for both teams.

The referees seemed to blow their whistles for no apparent reason, constant bad calls, but each team refused to become discouraged or thwarted by them.

The buzzer sounded for halftime. The Vikings were losing by six points. It was no secret—either pick it up or lose this game. The teams left the floor to the sounds of cheering and applause, but entered the locker room, to silence. No one said a word.

"Come on fellas, pump it up!!" roared Coach, pacing back and forth, clapping his hands. "This is no time to play sloppy basketball. You will lose this game."

"That giant is on me, Coach; I've tried all my moves to shake him, but it's like he won't get up off of me," said Chris, clearly frustrated.

"Do not lose your cool. That's what they expect," Coach replied sternly. "All of you need to stay focused; remember you are the best in this league!"

The entire team was pacing back and forth trying to regain their composure, downing drinks to quench their thirst and wiping the sweat off of their brows.

The whistle blew for the second half.

The minutes seemed to fly by as the Vikings ran back onto the floor to shoot around. The crowd chanted harmoniously, "D-fense, D-fense." The energy was even higher. It was now or never.

The inbound pass went to Boom. He turned, stepped back, and threw up a three-pointer. It went in and the crowd went wild. The team was filled with a new sense of hope. And play, they did.

The next two quarters were a fierce battle of experience and skill. Kai inbounded the ball and the opposing team stepped in, cutting Jay off and taking it all the way to the hoop for an easy lay-up.

"Stay focused!" yelled Coach from the sideline.

The crowd was filled with excitement on both sides of the gym. The cheerleaders cheered, the band played and anxious family members shouted words of encouragement from the stands.

With two minutes to go and the game tied, Coach called a time out.

"Let me tell you something. You need to play like your life depends on it. You see those young men on that team? They want to win just as bad, but you have one thing they don't: the home court advantage. Look around this gym. This is it for some of you: your last game and you have two minutes to get it done. We are the Vikings! So what is it gonna be gentlemen? Are you gonna just give that trophy away?"

"Look, we ain't walkin' outta here without that trophy. This is our court, and nobody's gonna come in here and take us down!" Boom said, with intensity. "Let's do this!"

"All right gentlemen, this is it. It's now or never."

Huddled together, they placed their hands in the middle, giving each other that one final look of encouragement. For a moment nothing mattered. Chris stood up and looked around the gym. Everything went into slow motion. It would be his final game here, and it was bittersweet.

Glancing into the stands, he thought about how his family's lives would never be the same. Then he thought about Mattie, the little girl who changed his life.

As the referee blew the whistle, the Monarchs inbounded the ball, but a costly error caused them to blow an easy lay-up.

Boom smiled at the team. The error would prove to be a costly one. He took it down the court and pulled up, shooting a quick two points from the top of the key.

Jerry got the ball after a quick steal. The Monarchs were losing their cool, and their lead. Coach called a wide screen for Jay, but a slip up allowed them to steal and go up for another two.

The Vikings regained their composure, pulling a couple of nice moves and tying the score.

A hush fell over the crowd. It was now or never.

Coach signaled for Boom to hold back. They had been practicing a new play that the team had not been able to complete. It required Chris to go airborne and dunk. The rest of the team saw Coach make the signal, but were shocked.

What is Coach thinking—in a championship game? The entire team questioned the play, but they fell into place.

Jay inbounded the ball to RJ. Grabbing it, he spun around faking a short jumper; he lobbed it off the backboard to Boom.

I need a miracle, Chris thought.

Time seemed to slow down.

The crowd was on their feet as the clock ticked down …4…3… Boom jumped up, meeting the ball midair as it bounced off of the backboard …2… Grabbing the ball with both hands, he slammed it down as the buzzer went off.

"BOOM!" the crowd yelled, and the announcer screamed.

The game was over. He had finally made his dunk.

Chris stood in shock as the team emptied the bench.

Time stood still; he had closed his eyes as he let the ball go. Opening them, he couldn't hear any words coming from the mouths of the people headed towards him. The excitement on their faces assured him that he must have made it. Quickly glancing up at the scoreboard, he saw his dream had become a reality.

The energy was incredible. The announcers were hoarse from screaming. It was unbelievable: the Vikings had finally beaten the Monarchs.

The team grabbed Boom, hoisting him up to cut down the net, while family and friends pushed their way through the crowd as they chanted and yelled.

After short hugs and accolades the team hurried into the locker room to prepare for interviews, photos and receiving the trophy. It would be a night of celebration and preparation for their next crossroad. Graduation.

Graduation Day

Chris woke up extra early and lay in bed thinking about the weeks before and the day ahead. Graduation morning was filled with a mixture of feelings and emotions. With a big stretch he got up and stared at himself in the mirror for about ten minutes. Suddenly he was overcome with nervousness, and unable to figure out why.

Today is the last day that I'll be going to high school, he thought, and then I'll be leavin' home.

He got dressed quickly and headed down the hallway; he could hear the normal noise coming from the kitchen. As he turneding the corner, Sydnee jumped out, startling him. "Surprise!" screamed his family.

He was standing in a room filled with balloons, and several beautifully wrapped gifts on top of the coffee table. He was speechless and had to catch his breath.

For a moment no one said anything. The only sounds in the room were a faint noise from the television, and Tina sniffling, trying to hold back tears.

Then Sydnee yelled.

"Come on, get it over with, so he can move out and I can get the bigger room," she said animatedly, dancing around the room.

"You shut up, girl. You ain't gettin' my room," Chris replied jokingly. "Tell her Ma, ain't no way, youngster, 'cause I'm not movin' to the campus. I'm gonna be staying home," he said, winking at Maurice.

"No! No way," she shouted, her voice filled with distress. "This ain't right! You and daddy promised me and—"

"Girl, be quiet," interrupted Maurice shaking his head. "Mom and I have something to say to Boom."

Tina had begun to cry, which changed the energy in the room. Sydnee watched quietly.

"I am so proud of you, Boom. And even though you won't be that far away, things will be different," Tina said sadly, "I won't get to see you as much and I'm gonna miss our late night talks and—" She began to choke up.

"I'm gonna miss taking you to the hole, boy," Maurice continued.

Sydnee stood silently her eyes beginning to well up.

"You make me sick," she said solemnly, wanting to reach out and grab him. "I don't know what to do."

"I love you too, Syd," said Chris tenderly.

He walked over to where she was standing and grabbed her in a bear hug. Emotions in the house were running high and tears of joy flowed freely.

After a few minutes Chris excused himself and ran down the stairs. He wanted to talk to Mattie before he left for graduation practice. They had not spoken to one another since the championship.

He took each step slowly, one by one, intently looking at each crack and crevice in the walls. The stroll down felt different this time. As he rounded the wall, he noticed Mattie sitting in a new spot directly in front of her door.

"Hey Mat, whatcha doin' over there?" he asked curiously.

"Things are changin', and we gotta be ready to move when change comes," said Mattie, fondly. "You reckon you have any changes comin'?"

"Yeah, but I'm not sure I'm ready," Chris said, squatting down next to her. "I'm gon' be leavin' in a minute for my graduation. You comin'?"

"Well I can't make any promises, Chris, 'cause I got some things to do and gon' be leavin' shortly, and I won't be back for a while," said Mattie, looking carefully through her notebook.

Chris's stomach twisted.

"What you mean that you won't be back? You'll be here tomorrow, right?"

Chris hesitated. He wasn't sure of what to do next.

Mattie opened her door and looked back at Chris who was staring blankly. "You have a great day, Boom, we'll see you soon. And remember to wake up your dreams."

Chris looked at her in surprise, started to say something, then stopped and swallowed hard.

Not sure of what to make of the interaction between the two of them, he continued to stand there while she quietly closed the door.

"Mattie," Chris whispered, tapping lightly on the door. "Are you there?"

There was silence. After a couple of seconds Mattie reappeared, smiling beautifully.

"You still here? You better get on to school. This is the biggest day of your life," said Mattie chuckling.

"I know, but are you gonna be around when I get back, or are you leaving for good? What's up?"

Mattie cleared her throat and in a maternal sounding voice, she said, "I got to finish some other work I started, and besides you have learned everything that you needed to know. There is nothing else for me to do. My job here is done, don't you think?"

"Well, ummm, I guess so…"

"So go on, and I'll see you again when I'm supposed to," said Mattie.

Chris stared blankly. He smiled sincerely and stepped backward toward the sidewalk and began kicking small rocks against the curb.

"Thanks, Mattie Fitch. And when I make it to the NBA, I'm gonna buy you something real special, you watch and see."

"I will be watchin', yes indeed."

Overcome with gratitude he walked towards her, leaned in and hugged her tightly.

"Thank you, Mattie," he whispered.

Turning quickly, he walked away never looking back. It was a long ride to school.

The students were antsy; they just wanted the graduation to be over so they could get on with the summer break. As the principal announced that they could transfer the tassels, the students went wild.

Chris walked eagerly towards his family who were visibly excited. "Hey Boom, congratulations honey," said Tina joyfully.

"Thanks Ma, Maurice.

"Well what do we do now?" asked Sydnee sarcastically.

"We are going to take you home so your brother can go out and enjoy his evening," replied Maurice.

After brief hugs and kisses Chris enthusiastically exited the scene surrounded by a crowd of well-wishers and hopeful girls.

About three o'clock in the morning, Chris arrived back at home, feeling both excited and exhausted from all of the after-graduation festivities. As he walked toward the building he noticed an envelope taped to Mattie's front door, addressed to him. There was a beautiful sunflower in the corner. Approaching slowly he caught the scent of lavender from the night breeze.

There was a sickening feeling in his stomach. He knew she was gone.

Snatching the envelope down from the door, he squatted against the wall clinching the letter tightly in his hand.

As he began to tear the envelope open thoughts raced through his mind and beads of sweat began to form on his brow. He read slowly.

Dear Chris,

It was a pleasure to meet you. Sorry I didn't get to say good-bye but there was some business somewhere else that I needed to attend to. You did well with yourself, and you will always be my friend. I want you to read everything you can get your hands on. It is the greatest gift we could ever receive besides love. You play good basketball, and every time you slam dunk it, be grateful.

Don't forget to be true to yourself always. No more secrets. Time waits for no man. You should always do your best to become what you are supposed to, so that the world doesn't miss out on what you have to offer.

You will become a player in the NBA if that is truly what you intend to do. Ask for what it is you want. Look for it in the smallest of places, and you will find it. I believe in you. On June 11, 2013 meet me directly in the middle of JL Square by the pier, at exactly 12 noon; I will have something for you. Until then, "your dreams are your reality asleep, wake up.

Your Friend,

Mattie Lee Fitch

His legs gave way to the weight and he plopped down holding the letter tight as he stared off into the black darkness. He felt tightness in his throat as he tried unsuccessfully to fight back tears.

She could have said goodbye, he thought. Things can only go up from here.

Chapter 6
North of the Border

It was like a family reunion. Everyone was there.

The streets of downtown were alive with color, laughter and sounds of mariachi bands playing patriotic songs. Accompanying dancers engaged in traditional Mexican folk dances. The women wore beautifully colored dresses, while the men accented them with their authentic western clothing. It was the fifth of May, 2008, Cinco de Mayo, the independence of Mexico emerging victorious from a battle with the French!

The sweet aroma of mole, tamales, menudo and a vast array of foods filled the air. A variety of vendors stood in their booths that lined the streets, offering a complete representation of Mexican cuisine. Men, women and children from all walks of life embraced the celebrations taking place around them. Flags of red, white and green flew gracefully in front of every home, store and restaurant, showing their true sense of pride and patriotism; it was a true festive atmosphere.

The excitement could be felt throughout. The sounds of bells, whistles, rattles, and the energy that flowed from the passing parade could be seen on the faces of the impatient children sitting along the curb. Everyone was gathered near the edge of the street eagerly anticipating catching some of the treats that were being tossed into the crowd.

Inside the Luna residence, they were preparing for their yearly performance. The stage had been beautifully decorated with strings of colored lights and magnificent flowers, as the crowd waited patiently for the show to begin.

"Can I do one of the other dances this year? I'm sick of doing just these dances," Veronica said, with frustration in her voice.

"Today is Cinco de Mayo, Veronica, so today you dance for your history," Angelina responded, surprised. "You have plenty of time to do all of that later."

"Mama, I'm seventeen and I want to dance on Broadway," she replied quickly. "And make lots of money. I'm sick of living in the 'hood. You don't know what I put up with," rolling her eyes.

Angelina, shook her head not sure how to respond.

"Nothing in life is easy Veronica," brushing Veronica's hair back into a braid. "We have a much better life since coming to America, and you should be happy that you have beautiful dresses and shoes, Veronica," she insisted.

"I want more, Mama," looking anxious. "Maybe I should just give in and join the gangs. I don't know how you and papa can be happy just workin' in this restaurant everyday, with nothin' to show for it," plopping down in the chair. "Did you ask Papa about the place next door?"

"Yes Veronica, but we will have to wait a little longer. The money is not available," Angelina hesitated. "And you want more? This is more than we've ever had, and I feel sad that you are not happy with this life. It could always be worse than this, remember that. Do not speak about gangs, Veronica. We have lost too many family members already," she replied solemnly. "We did not come here to lose our children to that life. It is not worth it. I will speak to papa after the show, and we will check on the place next door."

"It'll be gone soon. It's perfect for a dance studio," Veronica replied aggravated. "If you don't have the money now, you won't have the money later. Just forget it!"

"I understand, my love," Angelina said painfully, "but right now we need to go and do this performance, and then we can talk later. Okay Veronica? Please, no problems today," she pleaded.

"Yeah, yeah. It's always the same. But one day I will dance like I want." She grabbed her shawl. "Come on, Mama, let's go dance," she said sarcastically.

Just below their apartment, right next door to the restaurant was a vacant space. It was the perfect size for a dance studio, not to just fulfill her dreams as a dancer, but to provide an escape from the secret chaos that was following her, daily.

The windows of the building were partially covered with bits and pieces of newspaper. Veronica would peek in through small tears in the paper covering the windows everyday after school. She would stand looking, hoping and dreaming, sometimes for hours. Veronica would imagine herself on stage doing ballet, jazz and hip-hop; all of the dances she was learning in school. But it wasn't the same. Something had to change.

Veronica and Angelina entered the living room while Juan, Luis and Jesus, all dressed in the traditional garments of the mariachi. Juan walked over and took a quick look out of the window.

"The crowd is growing, let's get ready," he said excitedly.

They picked their instruments, and costume accessories and headed out of the door, as Angelina and Juan took up the rear.

"Juan, slow down for a minute, I need to talk to you," she whispered.

"What is it?" he responded.

"We must do something quickly. I am worried that our children are becoming the prey of gangs, Juan, and if we are not able to provide other things they will choose that life. Then what will we do?" she said. "I think we should have stayed in Jalisco."

"Do not worry about that right now, Angelina. We made the right choice. Our children would have never been able to live this way if we had stayed there. I believe in our children, and they will make the right choices. We will do what we can to give them what they need," he responded firmly.

As they walked out of the door, Veronica was looking curiously up at them from the bottom of the stairs, motioning frantically for them to come down.

"Hurry up!" she yelled, what are you guys doing up there? We gotta go on." "Come on."

"All right, all right Veronica, we are coming, and behave yourself," yelled Juan as they moved toward her. "Let's go!"

Approaching the stage, an excitement fell upon the crowd as the Luna men took the stage. The people were clapping and cheering. Little ones were smiling happily after being hoisted upon the shoulders of the men to allow them a good look.

A moment later, Veronica entered from the side, adorned in a beautiful traditional red and green ruffled dress that swirled as she glided across the stage. She looked into the crowd. Suddenly her eyes filled with excitement while clapping her hands together, stomping rhythmically around the sombreros which lay proud on the stage. Veronica stopped, smiled and posed majestically in front of her brothers as they serenaded her. Clicking her castanets, she began tapping her shoes with the greatest of ease. The crowd roared with applause, cheering and yelling for more. She craved the attention, smiling kindly at the crowd who had come year after year to see the Luna family perform.

The entertainment was always amazing. After each show Veronica and her brothers would find themselves surrounded by young admirers. It had been another successful year for the Luna Family.

The young girls and boys gathered around, some standing on their tip-toes in anticipation of being able to ask questions, while admiring Veronica and her brothers. These times reminded her of their years back in Mexico when the tables had been turned. The excitement was contagious, but there had to be more.

Veronica, trying to give the admirers some attention, looked anxiously over her shoulder at Juan who was excitedly packing up their equipment. She was waiting for just the right moment to approach him and ask about the place next door. It was now or never.

After graciously excusing herself and thanking those who were still standing around, she turned and headed directly toward Juan.

"Papa, did Mama tell you that I wanted to talk to you about something?" her voice rattled with excitement. "It's just right over here."

Grabbing his arm, she pulled him quickly through the crowd coming to a stop directly in the front of the place next door. She stood tensely, her back to the window staring compassionately into the eyes of her father.

"Okay Papa. You know you have always wanted to dance, so what if I told you that we could take this building and clean it up and maybe open a dance studio for me, and if."

"Hang on a minute honey," interrupting here. "It looks like someone has been here Veronica," said Juan, eyebrows slightly raised. "Turn around and look."

"What?" she yelled out. "You have got to be kidding me!" We waited too long." She stared bitterly at her father.

There was a brief moment of silence as Veronica stood with her hands rested upon her hips like a baby lying on the shoulder of its mother.

"Maybe the owner is cleaning it up to sell. Don't get down just yet, my love, we will see," he responded, optimistically. "I know you have always wanted to dance, and I want nothing more for you than to have that dream. That is why we risked our lives to come here so that you and your brothers could have a chance to be whatever you want. We will see what happens in a day or two. Until then do not lose hope."

"Don't lose hope, Really? Whatever. Nothing good ever happens for me, I'm sick of it. You guys always tell us that, but when is something going to happen, Papa?? She asked hopelessly.

Angelina had been watching the interaction from a distance, peering cautiously over the top of the few people still standing around. After several minutes she approached apprehensively, looking slightly wary.

"Is everything okay?" she asked quietly, touching Veronica lightly on her shoulder and smiling nervously at Juan.

"No, it's the same ol' thang. Look Mama," Veronica pointed toward the window. "Someone is moving into my place. Now what am I gonna do!" her voice broke with frustration.

"Come on Veronica, let's go inside so you can change your clothes and we can talk," she stated, sympathetically. "Don't stand out here getting more and more upset— come now."

"Whatever, it doesn't matter anyway. Nothing good will ever happen to us. We're just poor Mexicans stuck in the 'hood," she said sarcastically.

Angelina took a quick look over at Juan who shook his head, and shrugged his shoulders in disbelief. Suddenly, she grabbed Veronica by the arm looking her in the eye.

"You do not have the right to speak such things to us, Veronica. We are doing the best we can for you, your father is working hard, day and night. This is not fair," Angelina said in disappointment.

Veronica looked up, eyes filling with tears. "What kinda life is this?" she said, disheartened. "We'll just be doin' the same ol' thang that we always do."

"You should not be so ungrateful. In time you will see, good things come to people who have the patience to wait," Angelina responded confidently. "Believe in us, but most of all in yourself. You must continue to dream."

"I'm tryin', for real, but it's not that easy to fight anymore. We don't have no money. We all work like crazy just to get by; I just don't dream anymore," she said earnestly. "What for? They don't ever come true for folks like us, and I'm runnin' out of options."

"What do you mean by that?" Angelina and Juan asked in unison, looking perplexed.

"Nothin', just forget it," she replied pessimistically.

And suddenly a gust of cold wind blew in and around the gathering as they stood staring in silence. The change in atmosphere caused everyone to begin dispersing, Juan and Angelina, both stood motionless, struggling to find the words that would give Veronica the peace she longed for. But feelings of disillusionment were beginning to overtake them.

"Come on, children. Get inside. Something strange is happening with the weather," he said suspiciously, staring into the distance at the beautiful red storm clouds. "Let's go."

They all headed up the stairs into the house.

No one spoke.

"Mama!" Veronica yelled, bursting through the front door of the restaurant, looking around frantically for Angelina, who ran out from the kitchen after hearing the commotion.

"Mama, you'll never believe what happened! Our dance troop was chosen to go and visit with the dancers from Harlem for the end-of-the-year rally. We practiced with them today and everything and they is the bomb!" she said excitedly.

"Calm down, Veronica. That is wonderful," Angelina responded, drying her hands on the apron.

"They are dancers from the Dance Theatre of Harlem, in New York City, and they were some of the best dancers I've ever seen. I'm telling you they were the bomb, exactly the kind of Dance Company I would like to perform with one day, and they have a scholarship program and everything," said Veronica, pacing around excitedly.

"Harlem, Veronica?, you are not African American," she replied proudly, "and New York, it is very far."

Veronica stood quietly at a loss for words, staring at her mother in both shock and confusion.

"Mama, are you serious? What are you talkin' about? It's not just for African Americans. They had dancers of all races with them. Anyway, tonight they are performing and I want you to go with me to see them." She reached in her pocket and unfolded a flyer. "It starts at seven o'clock."

"I'm not sure, Veronica. This is a busy night in the restaurant, and we all need to be here to work," she said through a trembling voice.

Juan watched quietly from the behind the grill, but stayed where he was.

"You know I have always wanted to dance; now I have a chance to learn a little bit from the best and you are saying something weird. This is why I can't dream of doing anything more," she stated both disappointed and frustrated. "I've got to deal with the gang members tryin' to recruit me everyday, and I'm tryin' to stay focused and do somethin' positive, then you come and say some crazy stuff to me. What do you want me to do?"

Veronica walked slowly to a table and sat down abruptly. Angelina looked over at Juan for support, and then walked over and sat down beside her.

"Okay. Calm down. I did not mean it like that, but if it means that much to you, I will go," she said looking perplexed. "I will have your brothers come and help Papa. It will work out, and no more talk about gangs, Veronica. That is not good and will only bring trouble to our family. Please, okay, no more."

"For real. Thanks Mama. I can't wait for you to see what I'm talking about. It'll be fun," said Veronica excitedly, her brown eyes twinkling. "You'll see what I mean. I am so excited."

Angelina sat looking defeated as Veronica kissed her mother gently on the forehead and waved enthusiastically at Juan as she exited the restaurant. They looked at one another. Both shrugged their shoulders and smiled wearily. Juan turned around and continued cooking.

The show was electrifying, the music was intense, and with each dance step choreographed perfectly, the energy grew. Through the entire program they were both on the edge of their seats. As Veronica sat, she imagined herself as one of the dancers on stage, moving and swaying from side to side to the beat.

Angelina was fixated on the performance, visualizing her daughter on stage carrying out such detailed and precise moves, and stopping to look over from time to time at Veronica, who sat trance-like. The music became more loud and dramatic, and the pulse could be felt deep down, each movement precise and timely. The dancers moved graciously, incredibly and impressively to the melodies, breathless.

As the show came to an end, the entire team of dancers entered from both sides of the stage to a round of thunderous applause.

Veronica slumped back in her seat, staring blankly at the stage. Angelina glanced over and saw tears welling up in her eyes.

"Are you okay, Veronica?" Angelina shouted over the noise of the crowd.

"I'm fine Mama. Isn't this the best? This is what I want to do!" she said, watching Angelina closely. "Come on, Mama, let's get out there. I want you to meet them."

Veronica reached down for her mother's arm helping her up.

The aisles were crowded with excited students and parents making their way into the foyer for a chance to take pictures with the dancers.

In the lobby, the premier dancers were doing a meet-and-greet. The flashing of camera lights and excited bystanders lined up sent chills down the back of Veronica's neck, just confirming her dream.

They stood, waiting patiently arm in arm.

"This is going to be me one day, you watch and see," she said confidently.

"I believe you, and that is my hope for you, my love," Angelina said hesitantly, watching Veronica out the corner of her eye. The excitement was no less great.

They made their way slowly to the front of the line where several of the dancers greeted Veronica by name. Filled with emotion, she introduced each one to Angelina, who graciously accepted a barrage of compliments they shared about Veronica's natural talent.

"You know, one of these days she could dance with us," said one of the dancers in a certain voice.

"Oh yes, absolutely, Mama, once she has had all the training she needs. Don't you agree?" replied another dancer, astutely.

"Thank you very much," Angelina said nervously. "We are very proud of her and I am sure one day she will dance like this."

"We will make sure she gets the paperwork and fills it out, honey, and then let nature take its course," laughed one of the dancers flamboyantly. "Harlem, here you come!"

At that moment, a very large man dressed in a suit and with the stub of a cigar resting on his lip entered the room from behind the side door and instructed the dancers that it was time to go. Waving goodbye, with towels wrapped around their perfectly toned bodies, they exited as quickly as they had danced and boarded the bus for the hotel.

It had been an enjoyable evening. The ride home was strangely quiet. Angelina and Veronica arrived back at the house to notice what they thought was light shining through small cracks in the paper covering the windows of the studio. Suddenly, in the blink of an eye it was dark. Neither one of them remarked, each thinking they had made a mistake.

Veronica's excitement continued as she entered the house, tossing her coat over the back of the chair and startling Juan, who had been asleep.

"Papa, look at this!" Veronica exclaimed, doing a spin.

"Is that how you will wow the audiences on the big stage, Veronica?" Juan said, smiling lovingly.

"That is my goal."

"No way," interrupted her brothers. "This is how she will do it."

They both quickly moved to the middle of the room spinning each other around. "Okay boys that's enough," Juan said, stepping in mid-flow. "Veronica, I am very happy you had a good time. I want you to tell me all about it in the morning, but it is late and we have a long day tomorrow."

"All right. Good night," she replied dryly.

The next morning Veronica burst out of her bedroom door and into the kitchen where her parents were preparing breakfast.

"Do you hear that noise? Someone is in that studio," she said excitedly.

Juan hesitated, "Oh, I know, Veronica. I heard them last night," glancing over at Angelina.

"What!" she said, her eyes wide with excitement. With unexpected anticipation, she paused for just a moment and turned for the door. "I don't know what it is, but I feel something good's gonna happen," she stated innocently.

"Wait a minute, Veronica. You can't just go down there. You don't know what is going on, and you should wait," said Juan in a serious tone. "I don't want you to be disappointed."

"I just want to see if I can see anything. Luis, come with me," she said motioning for her brother. "We'll be right back."

Juan and Angelina both nodded in acknowledgement, as they headed out of the door and down the stairs. Once at the bottom of the stairs, they just stood, as she bit gently on her thumbnail and looked at her brother nervously.

"Okay. Should I knock or try to peek inside?" she asked uneasily. "What if someone sees us?"

"Well, we won't know unless we do something. Let's just kick it open and burst in like this," Luis stated confidently, in his best Rambo pose.

"Sh! Be quiet! Somebody might hear us and stop playin' around. This is serious," she whispered.

Sweat began to well up on her forehead as she paced back and forth in front of the door, looking over at Luis who was leaning impatiently against the wall. The sound of work inside was all she could stand.

"That's it!" he said anxiously. "I'm going to knock if you won't do it. This is dumb, just standing here. Come on, do something."

"Okay, okay," she said, moving towards the door to knock. "Okay." She wrung her hands and wiped them on her pants as she exhaled deeply.

Suddenly, there was complete silence. Leaning in quietly, they placed their ears on the glass, and listened.

The sound of footsteps heading towards the door grew louder, and a feeling of panic overtook them. There was very little time to think. They turned, and ran as fast as they could past the restaurant and up the stairs and into the apartment. As they fell inside, Luis reached back and slammed the door.

"Oh my God," said Veronica, winded, in between laughs with Luis as they lay on the floor.

"What are you doing?" Juan asked, quickly. "Did you see anyone?"

"No, she punked out," laughed Luis.

"Shut up! I didn't punk out, and you got a lot of nerve. You ran, too," she replied. "We heard someone in there and then they started to come toward the door so we ran."

"Don't go down there again. Stay away. Do you hear me?" Juan said sternly. "If someone catches you, they may call the police and bring more trouble to our home."

"Hey, you don't have to tell me twice," Luis replied nonchalantly. "You gonna have to do it yourself next time."

"I'm not trippin', but that scared the mess outta me. But I'll see someone sooner or later."

Veronica couldn't wait to get out of school. Everyday there seemed to be something new going on inside the studio. But she was never able to see anyone there.

The days to come would prove to be different.

It had been a long week and her patience had grown thin. The gym was noisy and crowded with the normal group of kids, those who just wanted to check the dancers out while they rehearsed, and the others who had nothing to go home to.

Veronica sat quietly on the bleachers.

Off in the distance she could see a couple of the gang members congregating. She had been able to keep them at bay for quite some time but they were determined to jump her in. Suddenly Sleepy, one of the leaders, walked in and gave Veronica the nod. Sleepy was short, but her confidence made her tall. She wore her hair gelled back and thick black eyeliner which made her look crazy, but no one dared tell her. Her clothes were always baggy as if she was trying to hide something, and her eyes oozed a life of disappointment. Veronica looked away quickly and jumped down off of the bleachers and rejoined dance practice as if it was not meant for her, but she knew it was. Sleepy had been working overtime trying to recruit Veronica who had been, until now, focused on the future.

Practice was strangely grueling. Veronica found herself agitated, awkward and unable to stay focused; her mind was on the studio and trying to stay away from the gang. She didn't feel like her normal self.

Everyone was crowded around chatting about their weekend plans, while she concentrated on her plan to get inside that building, and how to get home without having to talk her way out of being jumped on. Her goodbye was quick, leaving her friends looking confused about her strange behavior. But time had run out, and she needed to get home.

Opening the gym door slowly and overcome with a sickening feeling, she scanned the perimeter closely to see if she could spot anyone, her heart pounding.

They're gone, she thought to herself, thank God. She exhaled a sigh of relief and pushed the door completely open and bolted down the walkway. Unbeknownst to her they had been watching from a distance and approached her as she prepared to cross the street.

"What up, Veronica? You kickin' it wit' us today or what?" Sleepy asked, leaning against the tree.

"Oh, hey, what up, Sleepy," Veronica responded. "I'm not going to able to do nothin'. My practice took too long and I gotta get home."

A car filled with other members pulled up next to the curb blasting its music.

Veronica cast an irritated eye towards the car as she turned back to face Sleepy, who was visibly irritated.

"You know you can't keep fakin', 'cause you ain't gon' have no choice in a minute," she replied harshly, both fists clenched.

At that moment an old brown station wagon with two mixed matched doors and a tiny crack in the windshield pulled up alongside the curb. Behind the wheel sat a visibly beautiful woman, her glasses perched on the tip of her nose, as she fumbled with a map.

Veronica and Sleepy stopped their conversation and looked over at the woman, in surprise.

Smiling elegantly through the dirty glass she leaned over and rolled down the window by hand.

"Hi, excuse me, but I was wondering if you could help me. I am trying to find this street," she asked, pointing to a small piece of paper.

Sleepy turned and ignored her, having begun to grow impatient.

"Um, sure I'll help you," Veronica stated quickly, moving toward the car.

"I don't think so, let's go," Sleepy said harshly, grabbing Veronica by the arm.

Suddenly the sounds of sirens heading towards the school caught their attention as Veronica snatched her arm out of Sleepy's grasp. They both looked across the street at the passengers motioning frantically for Sleepy to come toward the car.

"You better go. It looks like the sirens are for you guys and I'm gonna stay and help this lady," Veronica shrugged.

"I'll get with you later!" Sleepy yelled, wrinkling her brow. "You gotta do your thang eventually."

The sound of the sirens grew closer as the car sped away.

Veronica turned around, breathless. The woman in the car was gone and the street deserted.

I've got to get out of here, thought Veronica anxiously running across the street. She could barely remember walking home. The only thing that was on her mind was getting into the studio.

Approaching home, she had made the decision to get in that studio no matter what. She stopped dead. Slightly winded from previous excitement, she noticed the door was partially open.

Oh my God, someone is in there, she thought, frantically looking around to see if someone was watching as she ran full speed to the building. She paused, and leaned against the wall to catch her breath.

Several minutes passed.

It was now or never.

She carefully leaned in, placing her ear between the cracks of the door. There was silence.

"Hello," she whispered nervously, pushing the door open a crack at a time.

Veronica entered the room quietly. It was perfectly spotless.

Everything was placed exactly like she had imagined. It was just right. There was a calming aroma of lavender in the air. The first thing she noticed were several vases of sunflowers arranged modestly about.

Just inside the door was a medium-sized reception desk with a help wanted sign lying on top.

That's it, she thought excitedly, proceeding inside. I can say I'm here looking for a job!

She tiptoed in further, and then stopped to admire every element.

Two of the four walls were mirrored. Along the right wall was a ballet bar. Across the back of the room were shelves that were filled with a vast array of dance gear. Positioned perfectly in the corner was a stereo system. Adjacent to that was a small hallway.

I've got to get a closer look, Veronica thought nervously, creeping both slowly and quietly toward the hallway. As she approached the doorway, she noticed a set of stairs leading to the second floor, a bathroom at the end and a closed door with the word *Office* on the front.

Pausing, she admired her reflection in mirrors.

All at once she heard what sounded like someone from behind the office door. "Hello, is anyone there?" Veronica stated, both nervous and anxious. She walked toward the door.

No one answered.

She continued toward the sounds. Feelings of uneasiness filled her up. Her eyebrows rose as she stopped, looking cautiously from side to side. From underneath the door of the office she could see light, and the faint sound of singing.

"This little light of mine, I'm gonna let it shine….oh, this little light of mine, I'm gonna let it shine….

Panic set in. Her mind began racing with outrageous thoughts. What happens if someone grabs me, and I never see my family again? What if I get arrested? Get a hold of yourself, she thought confidently. It's now or never.

Stopping abruptly, she looked back over her shoulder one last time catching a glimpse of her reflection in the mirror. A sense of calm took over; there was nothing to fear, because the time was now.

"Hello," tapping lightly on the door. "I was wondering if you were still looking for someone to work here," she stated, nervously.

The singing stopped. There was silence.

What if it's some crazy person, she thought one last time.

The sound of a sliding chair and footsteps coming toward the door caused tiny beads of sweat to form on her brow. As she turned to run, the sound of a sweet voice replied, just in the nick of time.

"Just a moment, please," said a pleasant woman's voice from behind the door, "I'm coming."

Veronica stood anxiously.

Suddenly standing, to her surprise, was a stunning, tall and graceful African American woman. She appeared to be around thirty years old. Her brown wavy hair parted neatly down the center gave way to two thick black braids that crossed carefully around her head. Two thin black eyebrows separated a pair of piercing brown eyes that seemed to hypnotize you if you stared too long. Her smile was contagious; it left Veronica in awe.

"Well hello again, how are you?" she stated kindly, opening the door to greet Veronica who stood awestruck, her mouth slightly open. "Are you all right?"

"Oh yeah, I'm sorry. You caught me off guard," Veronica said, clearing her throat. "Didn't I just see you over at the school a little bit ago askin' for directions?" Veronica thought, in amazement.

"Well yes, indeed, you are absolutely right. Now what is your name, young lady?" she asked cheerfully.

Veronica stood staring in wonder.

"Oh, I'm sorry," giggling shyly. "My name is Veronica, but my family and friends call me Veronica."

"Well, ain't that somethin'! My name's Mattie," she responded, smiling expressively. "Come on in."

Veronica entered the office and took in everything around her. There were photos everywhere.

A beautiful wooden desk sat in the far corner with an oversized chair and a beautiful bouquet of sunflowers, and a peaceful aroma of something beautiful filled her nostrils. Directly behind the desk sat two file cabinets with blue labels and white writing, and right above them hung a poster board with hundreds of ticket stubs and programs.

"Did you dance at all of these places?" Veronica asked, pointing to the programs.

"Why yes, I did. But this is where my heart is," Mattie said excitedly, walking over to a photo of a beautiful home, with a field of sunflowers. "There is nothing like this. When you dream enough, you can be anywhere and do anything you want, you know."

"Yeah, I guess," Veronica said slightly puzzled. "Oh my God, you danced with them? They are my favorite!" she responded excitedly, after catching a glance of a poster of the Dance Theatre of Harlem. "I'm gonna dance with them one day! Well, I mean I want to dance with them one day, but the way my life's goin', I'm never gonna get to do anything."

"Do you dance?" Mattie asked.

"Yeah, I've been dancin' since I was about seven, but I always wanted to do more than just traditional Mexican dancin', so I took classes whenever and wherever I could, as long as they were free. And I pretty much taught myself to street dance. But I've always wanted to dance like this," she said, pointing to the poster. "Just a couple of days ago my school dance program hosted them. And once I got to see them in person, I knew for sure that is where I wanted to dance one day. I'm just getting tired of getting teased about wanting to dance professionally, and then knowing my parents expect me to stay close and help run our restaurant. Then my mom keeps telling me I have to remember where we came from, and keep dancing traditional Mexican dances. It's frustrating."

"You should never grow tired of where you come from."

"I love my heritage—don't get me wrong—and the dances of Jalisco, but it doesn't give you any money. That's why I'm here, to see if you need any help."

After a couple moments of silence, Mattie walked towards the door and motioned for Veronica to follow.

"Come with me, Veronica," Mattie stated gently.

They walked out of the office and down the dimly lit corridor into the studio. Mattie walked over to the stereo, looked back over her shoulder and smiled empathetically at Veronica, who was stood motionless.

All at once the beautiful sound of flamenco music blasted through the speakers. Veronica immediately started to shake her hips from side to side to the rhythm. She wanted to dance.

"How do you feel, Veronica?" Mattie asked inquisitively, her voice rising over the music.

"I feel good. Hearing that music always makes me feel like dancing," she responded innocently.

At that moment, both Mattie and Veronica's eyes met and they smiled at each other. Mattie grabbed the sides of the beautifully decorated skirt and began dancing. She glided across the floor rhythmically, systematically stomping and clapping in perfect unison.

Veronica stood frozen, watching in amazement as she moved gracefully, elegantly and flawlessly through the motions.

"Come on, child; let me see what you can do!" Mattie yelled out, reaching for Veronica to join her on the floor. "Come here." pointing to the spot on the floor next to where she was dancing.

"Right now?" she responded, looking around the room nervously.

"Right now, come on!" she repeated clapping her hands together loudly.

In a moment, they were dancing, spinning, clapping in perfect sequence. Veronica caught on quickly.

Mattie signaled Veronica with her eyes that it was time to end. Instantly they both took one final stomp as the music ended.

Winded and excited, they laughed joyfully, grabbing hands.

"Wow! That was a trip," Veronica said breathlessly. "You are so good, Mattie, I wanna dance like that all the time. I mean dancing is my dream, and my way out of this life, 'cause things are getting pretty bad around here with gangs and everything. We don't have a lot to choose from, you know?"

"You choose the path in which your life will go, Veronica. No one chooses for you," Mattie stated wisely. "Come on, sit, child."

They grabbed a couple of mats, sat on the dance floor and continued to talk. "Dreams are just your reality asleep. Wake up Veronica."

"Not around here Mattie. I didn't choose this life, my parents did, and unless something magical happens, this is where I'll be."

Mattie motioned to Veronica to move closer to her and she grabbed two bottles of water from a small refrigerator. They sat catching their breath for a moment, Mattie smiling.

"This would make a great place to practice dancing, don't you agree?" Mattie stated inquisitively, twisting the cap off the bottle.

"Oh my God yeah, that's why I'm here. I would dance everyday if I could, but between working with my folks, school and trying to stay away from the gangs, I don't have a lot of positive time, you know."

"Being a dancer takes a lot of discipline and focus, Veronica. There can be no excuses."

"Can you help me, Mattie? I'll do anything."

"You should never be willing to do anything, because there are some who may require you to settle. Never settle," said Mattie seriously. "How bad do you want to fulfill this dream?"

"I want it more than anything; it will be an opportunity to help my family, and to have some things that I really want, and to move away from this place."

"This place, what do you mean?"

"The 'hood, the ghetto, whatever you want to call it. I don't want to be here anymore," said Veronica with a tone of irritation.

"You will understand that you must find peace wherever you are, and home is simply a place where love should dwell, no matter the address."

"Where are you from, Mattie? Tell me a little about you," asked Veronica, taking a big gulp of water.

"I'm from a small town, Darlington, South Carolina," she said proudly. "I miss being home right now, but I have some business to take care of. But as soon as I'm done, I'm going right back there and see my family and friends. My family members are hard workers; we made part of our living sharecropping tobacco and selling vegetables at that market. And my Momma would make extra money cleaning a home on the property where we lived. I would help her from time to time, but I would always end up playing with my best friend, Pamela, who lived in the home. I sure do miss her right now."

Suddenly Mattie stopped.

Veronica took a swig of water and sat back in amazement.

"I've talked enough and it's getting late, and besides if you're going to be working with me, you'll need plenty of rest and time to do all of your schoolwork and chores," Mattie said.

"Can we dance just a little more?" Veronica begged.

"Don't worry, Veronica, we will have plenty of time for dancing, and you will find that it will come naturally for you. Once you make the decision that nothing will stop you from your goal, doors will open, you'll see."

In excited anticipation she jumped up, gathering the mats and towels, putting them neatly in their place.

"Thanks, Mattie, but you don't even have to worry. I will get everything done and be on time everyday. I can't mess this up," said Veronica excitedly yet somberly.

"Veronica, we all have something that we are supposed to do, and you have realized what your gift is. There are so many young people who no longer choose to believe in their gift, so they spend most of their time chasing nothing and going nowhere."

"I know, it's sad that most of the kids I know who are really talented, you know with art or music, they end up joining gangs or doing drugs and getting pregnant 'cause they don't see no way out. That's why I decided no matter what I had to keep dreaming, and one day my prayers would be answered."

They approached the door and Mattie opened it slowly. They both stood there looking out into the streets. Veronica exhaled deeply and stepped out onto the sidewalk.

"Mattie," Veronica said quickly. Mattie prepared to close the door.

"Yes, child?"

"You saved my life,"

Suddenly she grabbed Mattie and hugged her tightly. "Am I dreaming?" she said, as her eyes filled with tears.

"Oh no child, don't worry. We have only just begun," said Mattie warmly, squeezing her tightly and kissing her lightly on the forehead. "Good night, child, sleep well; oh, and I will see you at 5pm."

"Yes you will!" she replied. "Good night, Mattie."

The door closed lightly.

She floated through the doors of the restaurant. "I've got a secret," she sang out, looking at her parents who were posted behind the counter.

"Where have you been, Veronica? We expected you long ago and we were starting to worry." Angelina asked, slightly irritated.

"Well, I met the person next door, her name is Mattie and she is gonna let me work there part time and give me professional dance lessons." she smiled.

"We must meet this Mattie, if you are to be spending time there, Veronica," Juan interrupted.

"Okay, okay. You can go over there tomorrow," Juan and Angelina said.

"Well, we have closing to do 'cause it's getting late."

Veronica half-turned and began cleaning tables. "I wanted to surprise you, but its okay; I'm going to show you."

"Tomorrow is a new day!"

Mattie met Veronica at the door, smiling widely. It was as if she was already expecting her.

"Hi, Miss Mattie, have my parents come by here today? They wanted to meet you and—"

"Bring them on over, right now; I would love to meet them," Mattie interrupted,

nicely.

"Oh okay, I'll go get them," said Veronica, slightly surprised. She put her backpack down and went toward the restaurant, reappearing moments later with her parents.

"Mattie, these are my parents, Juan and Angelina." Mattie smiled. "They wanted to meet you and see if I was telling the truth."

"Oh, Veronica, stop it," Angelina stepped in. "We just wanted to make sure that she was not bothering you," Angelina said, as she extended her hand to shake. "And that, well," clearing her throat, "that she was telling us the truth." Angelina smiled, shamefully.

"She is a wonderful young lady with lots of potential," said Mattie. I am looking forward to working with her, and y'all feel welcome to come on over anytime."

The three of them continued to talk while Veronica fell into deep thought for a moment.

Things were about to change.

Every day she made her way to the studio, talking and dancing for what seemed like hours. Even once they had finished practicing for the night, she just wanted to sit and talk with Mattie.

"Mattie, tell me more about your life," Veronica asked.

"Oh child, I come from a small town in South Carolina, not much goes on there, but we got lots of love flowin'."

"Well, tell me more about how you learned to dance."

Mattie didn't feel much like talking about her past. She always seemed to be able to sidestep the questions because once the people she helped started asking too much she knew it would be time to leave.

Mattie hesitated. "Well, I think I told you about my best friend Pamela back home." She said as she wiped her forehead with a towel. "Well, shes taught me to dance and once I got a taste of it I just couldn't stop."

"I am so happy that you came," Veronica replied warmly, smiling widely, "because if you hadn't come I would still be just sittin' around dreamin'.

Mattie looked amused. "I am right happy to be able to help you live out your dreams."

Mattie stopped for a moment and looked around the room, caught up in a memory of home, and a faint smell of lavender filled the studio.

"It was my mama who used to say that dreams are just your reality asleep—wake 'em up. That's just what you have to do."

"I know," said Veronica, "and because of you I'm gonna dance hard and as much as I can. I need to make my family proud and you Mattie. I don't think I can thank you enough for being there. I still think about that day when you just showed up, right on time and my life hasn't been the same since."

"Don't credit me Veronica. You had it in you the whole time; I just helped to open the door, and you stepped through," Mattie said. "Now, let's pack up because you have a big day comin' tomorrow, and you need a good night's sleep so that you can wow those judges."

"You're right," Veronica replied coolly. "I gotta be ready."

Veronica gathered her things and shoved them in her backpack that she slung over her shoulder as she headed for the door. Mattie sat quietly watching her muddling about and smiled lovingly. "Good night child."

"Good night, Mattie, and thanks." Veronica blew a kiss and shut the door.

The Audition

They pulled into the parking lot; there were cars everywhere. Juan pulled into a vacant spot and stared blankly in the rearview mirror. He managed an innocent smile. "Are you ready, Veronica?"

"Yes, but I'm feelin' a little sick to my stomach." She rolled down the window and inhaled deeply. The day she dreamed of had finally arrived. It was pleasant, calm, with a warm breeze. She was confident in her ability, but butterflies had taken up residence in the pit of her stomach. *Your dreams are just your reality asleep — wake up.* Mattie's words of encouragement and support rang loudly in her ears as she opened the car door. They walked quickly down the concrete walkway while the the tap of Angelina's shoes echoed off the brick walls. As Veronica opened the door, she saw people everywhere, stretching, spinning, and practicing their moves.

Suddenly the butterflies in her stomach began to feel stronger, and the confidence turned into nervousness.

"These girls are professionals. I can't do it," she said frantically, looking back at her parents.

"Yes, you can," they said quickly, in unison.

"Go, Moreno," Angelina said softly. "We will be waiting for you."

"I wish Mattie was here," Veronica said wistfully.

"She is here in spirit, she has trained you well. Now go, and believe in what you have learned," Juan responded firmly.

They closed the door leaving Veronica by herself. She began scanning the room looking for a friendly face to help bring her back to the reality.

Then she could hear the sweet whisper of Mattie's voice in her mind. *Veronica, you are wonderfully made, don't be afraid. I am right there with you. You can do anything.*

Instantly the sense of nervousness eased and feelings of confidence rose up like a warrior headed to battle. It was now or never.

Veronica took a deep breath then opened the door and peeked inside the room where the judging would take place. At the far end of the room sat a long table with six elegantly written nameplates white folders lying adjacent.

Veronica moved back, closing the door quietly; she closed her eyes, squeezing them shut.

"Crazy huh?" said one of the participants.

Startled, she opened her eyes quickly. "Oh, you scared me!" Veronica giggled nervously. "Yeah, this whole thing is crazy."

"My name is Trish; I came all the way from Seattle to audition. What about you?"

"My name is Veronica; I'm from right here in LA."

"Oh, cool, you have to go down there and get signed in," Trish said, pointing to another table at the end of the hallway where a serious looking woman sat staunchly. "I'll save you a spot so you can stretch."

"Thanks. I'll be right back," said Veronica.

She arrived at the table and handed the woman her papers and continued to smile anxiously at the others standing around trying to look confident. She was considering what to do next when a portly man swung open the door to the audition and called the first person. It had begun.

Taking a deep breath she walked back to where Trish was sitting, slid down the wall and began to stretch.

"It seems as if everything is going in fast motion, but I need to make this, girl, for real," said Trish, stretching.

"I know me too, but I wish you the best. How long you been dancin'?"

"Man, seems like forever, but since I was around six."

"Wow, me too. I—"

The portly man reappeared.

"Number 10, it's time," he scowled.

"That's you, boo!" Veronica bellowed with excitement.

Trish got up, turned around and slapped Veronica a high five.

"It's now or never, chica. I'll see you in New York!"

Veronica grinned and gave her the heads up, as she disappeared behind the door.

After what seemed like forever the portly man reappeared and finally called her number.

Veronica entered the room quietly but gracefully, making sure each judge had time to get a good look at her. Approaching the table, she greeted each judge with a firm handshake and self-confident smile, just like Mattie had instructed.

Handing her music to the engineer she nodded politely. "I'm ready," she whispered. "Let's begin."

She hesitated. But the sound of the music seemed to take over her body, moving rhythmically from the top of her head to the soles of her feet. It was an out-of-body experience. It felt good, real and right.

When the smoke cleared, the judges sat speechless behind the table at the end of the room, smiling slyly and clapping modestly. Veronica was not altogether sure what the cryptic smiles meant, but she was confident that her presence had been made known.

"Thank you," said Veronica breathlessly.

A petite female judge, who sat auspiciously at the end of the table stood up, cleared her throat, raised her eyebrows expectantly, and then licked her lips as if her mouth was dry. "Thank you, Miss Luna. If we decide you are what we are looking for, you will hear from us in about one week."

Nodding kindly, her eyes smiling, she was excused.

Veronica, her face hot, hair wet and smile wide, was overcome with excitement as she pushed passed the others dancers and outside to her parents, who were nervously waiting for her to emerge.

Suddenly her body gave way to the overwhelming surge of emotions she had held in and collapsed into the arms of her tearful mother who gave a reassuring smile.

"I bet you were the best dancer ever, Veronica," whispered Angelina.

"Say something, Veronica," said Juan, his voice heavy with worry. "How did it go?"

"I believe in my heart I did it, I'm gonna get in," she replied, her voice quivering. "They said I would find out next week, but Mattie told me about people that have heard before then, so I'm hoping that happens to me."

"Well, don't be disappointed if you don't hear right away. Just plan to hear when they said," Angelina said opening the car door. "But if you hear before then, that is even better. But one thing we want you to know is that you were right, it doesn't matter where you go to dance as long as you find happiness when you get there."

"You mean that, for real?" asked Veronica, surprised.

"Yes, we do," they answered delightfully, in unison.

Veronica got in the car and nestled into the backseat, replaying the day over in her mind 'til she dozed off.

She finally woke up and in the distance the colorful lights of the city were just coming into view on the horizon. Again, excitement filled her body. As they got closer to home she could see that the lights were on in the studio. Mattie was there.

"Hurry up, Papa, you're driving so slowly," said Veronica in a tone of desperation.

"Calm down, my love, we're here," replied Juan.

Suddenly, before the car could come to a complete stop, Veronica leaped out running full speed toward the studio.

"Mattie," yelled Veronica, knocking on the locked door. "Mattie, are you here?"

"Just a moment," said Mattie calmly. "I'm coming."

As Mattie opened the door, Veronica was greeted with a smile of confidence.

"Well, how did it go?" said Mattie, motioning for Veronica to enter the studio.

"Mattie, you won't believe how well I did. I was nervous but I handled my business, and at the end this one lady stood up and said if they liked me they would call in a week, just like you said, Mattie," Veronica rattled off without taking a breath.

Mattie stopped and looked at Veronica proudly. "There was never a doubt in my mind that you would be capable of success, you just needed to believe in yourself."

Veronica began to pace back and forth admiring herself in the mirror. "I remember when I use to think I would never be able to dance in a real studio, or even get accepted into a dance theater," she whispered.

Mattie watched Veronica for a moment and turned her attention to a pile of boxes stacked in the corner.

"There never seems to be enough time," said Mattie somberly.

Veronica's eyes widened. "What are you doing," she asked nervously.

"I have to take a trip. Things are very busy this time of the year," replied Mattie, picking up one of the boxes and placing it on the table.

Veronica's eyes widened. "Where are you going?"

"I have to go away for a bit, but don't worry, you will see me again," said Mattie nonchalantly.

"Will you be here for my graduation, and at least to make sure I got in the dance school? I don't understand," said Veronica, sliding one of the boxes with her foot, pushing it towards Mattie, clearly annoyed.

Mattie, who always radiated a sense of calm, smiled and continued to write on the box with a huge black marker, humming gracefully. After a minute she paused and looked over at Veronica, who had walked to the pile of boxes.

"There are times that you will not understand everything, but believe that you have overcome the obstacles that were holding you hostage," said Mattie maternally. "And you don't need me to hold your hand. You are quite capable."

"It isn't like I want you to hold my hand or anything," said Veronica glumly. "I'm just surprised you're just taking off like that. I wasn't expecting it, that's all."

"I know, but you will learn that there are some people that enter our lives for only a season," said Mattie kindly, "and they move on, having made a difference.

Veronica hesitated and then walked over to Mattie. "I mean, I will see you again, right?"

Mattie could see that Veronica was hurt, and spoke quickly to ease the fear that had risen up in her eyes.

"Of course," said Mattie, hurriedly putting the marker down on one of the boxes. She took a hold of Veronica's hand and pulled her near, giving her a gentle embrace. "When the time is right."

They stood for just a moment with Veronica's head resting peacefully on Mattie's shoulder. A moment later the telephone rang. Mattie politely excused herself to take the call. She emerged a few moments later.

"Veronica, this is an important call and I will be a while longer so I must say good night, but we will talk tomorrow," said Mattie apologetically.

"Oh, okay it's cool. I'll see you tomorrow."

Veronica stood and watched as Mattie disappeared into the hallway, closing the door to her office with its normal loud thump. There was a lump in her throat that wouldn't go down no matter how hard she swallowed. The lights on the sign out in front seem to dim slightly, and the air in the studio didn't feel quite the same. Veronica went to the door and opened it. Suddenly her legs started to tremble and she remembered how hard the day had been, and how tired she was. *I had a great audition,* she thought, *and I guess it's up to me now to figure out where to go from here.*

Veronica shook off the blues and headed upstairs. She knew there would be joy waiting.

The week had been long and tiring. Everyone was preparing for graduation but, more importantly, Veronica had the anxiety of waiting for the letter or phone call which eventually became unbearable.

Walking home she could see her mom in the distance laughing with the postman in front of the restaurant, a large manila envelope in her hand.

It's the dance school! She thought.

"Mama," she yelled, running in a full stride, waving her arms frantically, "is it the school?"

"Yes, my love, come hurry!" Angelina replied excitedly, waving the envelope back and forth.

Veronica snatched the envelope from Angelina's hands and proceeded into the restaurant, full stride. She tossed her backpack and jacket onto an empty chair and stopped, breathing deeply, holding on tightly to the envelope.

"Oh my God, Mama, Papa, come see!"

Juan emerged from the kitchen, eyes wide with excitement. "What's going on?"

"The letter is here! I can't believe it." Veronica stopped mid-sentence looking as if she had seen a ghost.

"What's wrong?" Angelina asked.

"What if it's bad news? I don't think I could take it!"

"Calm down girl, and open the letter," said Juan. "That is the only way to find out what their decision is."

"Okay, okay," she laughed.

Juan and Angelina moved in close to watch quietly while Veronica began tearing at the envelope, her hands shaking slightly. "I can't open it, I am starting to feel sick," she said nervously. At that moment she heard Mattie's voice of confidence speak quietly: *Veronica, there is no need to worry. Open the envelope child.*

She opened the envelope quickly, pulling out the letter and reading frantically, "Oh my God, I got in!" she yelled in excitement. "Mama, Papa, I got in!"

Joy filled the room.

"There was never a doubt in our minds," both exhaled in unison.

The next morning, Veronica jumped out of bed, excited, as she prepared for her graduation. As she stared in the mirror, her reflection was different. This time there was an aura of confidence that radiated all around her.

She would be heading off to New York City to begin the life of her dreams: to dance. In the house, she could hear the sound of happiness and smell the fragrance of her favorite traditional foods being prepared. The sweet aroma of fresh tortillas and enchiladas baking, and a vast array of herbs and spices blending harmoniously in the air, caused Veronica to choke back tears.

She opened her bedroom and overheard Juan Jr. and Luis laughing while they talked back and forth about which one would get her bedroom once she was gone. Veronica turned on her heel laughing to herself, capturing a final glance in the mirror.

"Good morning, graduate," Angelina said happily. "Are you hungry?"

"Not really," she replied. "Just thinking about how soon after the graduation I have to leave for New York."

"Well, you could just stay here and work in the restaurant," Juan said humorously.

"I don't think so, Papa."

"Hey, have you talked to Mattie?" Angelina interrupted.

"No," Veronica shrugged. "I'm gonna go and see if she is around in a little while."

After the graduation, Veronica was fidgeting in the backseat as if she needed to use the bathroom.

"What are you doing back there?" Juan said quickly, looking in the rearview mirror.

"I just wanna get home and see if Mattie's there," she responded cheerfully.

"I bet she ain't there," said Juan Jr. sarcastically.

"Shut up boy, you make me sick," Veronica scowled.

She didn't want to admit it but the thought had already crossed her mind and it was the last thing she needed or wanted to hear.

With a wry smile, Juan Jr. said, "Well I'm just sayin' that she might be gone."

"Well, either way we want to think positive," Angelina interjected.

A very long silence followed, and Veronica continued to stare out of the window and lapsed into a daydream. She was quickly disturbed by the sound of Juan yelling, "There's a closed sign on the door!"

"What!" asked a startled Veronica?

"Look!" Juan responded with concern.

It took her a moment to gather herself as she looked toward the dance studio and focused on a sign posted on the door, **CLOSED.** A large lump in her throat nearly cut off her breath as she slumped down in the seat.

"Veronica," Angelina spoke softly, "I am sure she will be back."

"No," said Veronica quietly, "I knew she wouldn't be here, but I was hoping.

As the car came to an abrupt halt Veronica exited and walked over to the entrance of the studio and slid down the wall, never muttering a word, as the rest of the family entered the restaurant.

"Veronica?" Angelina said lovingly, and Veronica glanced up, her eyes glittered with tears.

"What is that?" Her voice strangled. She looked over to see Angelina holding a white envelope with *Veronica* written beautifully on the front. She got to her feet and nervously walked over to where Angelina stood in the doorway.

"She's gone, Mama," said Veronica, looking slightly alarmed.

Angelina nodded.

"I thought she would be here for the party, or at least wait and say goodbye."

She grabbed the envelope and began to open it slowly.

"I am sure she waited as long as she could. Read it."

"Ma, please," Veronica said dryly, "I just want to be by myself."

Veronica slid down the wall in her graduation garb and sat on the ground in front of the studio. This was a comfortable place where she had come many times to hope and dream. Holding tight to the letter she began looking around the neighborhood that had become home since leaving Mexico. For a few moments she studied her surroundings—the liquor store across the street, the two homeless men that had made the empty building overhang their home, and the faces of the beautiful people that had become victims of dreams still asleep. She smiled widely and began to read:

Dear Veronica,

First, let me begin by telling you what a wonderful, gifted dancer you are. Your dedication and commitment will take you farther than you could have ever imagined. I had to leave in a hurry because I am needed elsewhere and in time you will understand that we all have special gifts to offer the world.

You will dance for the world, if that is truly your heart's desire. Ask for what you want; look for it in the smallest places and you will find it.

The wonderful thing about life is that one day we will see each other again, and I look forward to that. On June 11, 2013, I want you to meet me directly in the middle of JL Square by the pier, at exactly 12 noon; I will have something for you. Until then......

"Your dreams are your reality asleep, wake them up."

Your Friend,

Mattie Fitch

Veronica stood up catching a quick glimpse in the reflection of the window. She froze, startled by what she thought was Mattie standing behind her, but it was simply her imagination—or was it? She took a deep breath, exhaled and headed inside.

Chapter 7
The Journey Begins

Everything was strangely quiet in the Fitch home that beautiful Saturday morning. There had been an unexpected storm the night before, and by the time the family awoke the rain had been replaced by a beautiful sunrise. The picturesque arrangement of colors blended together symbolically in that peaceful moment of stillness.

The Fitch's hadn't much to talk about since Mattie fell in the water and into the deep sleep. Those few days seemed like a lifetime.

The Doc had been around almost everyday looking into Mattie's sleeping eyes, and just digging in and out of his bag trying to look as if he was trying to do something. But nothing ever happened.

Each family member would take turns sitting and talking with Mattie. They tried to do whatever they could to rouse her from the cavern of blackness.

Almost nightly they would gather as a family around her bed and say a prayer; once Dozier and Leona were finished everyone walked quietly away, their heads hung low.

On this particular morning Leona had a strange feeling unlike anything she had ever felt before. Her stomach refused to allow anything more than a sip of hot black tea to enter it. She could barely anticipate the next breath. It had been almost two weeks that Mattie had gone to sleep. Leona felt like she had run out of tears, the ones that burn your eyes. But despite the sadness the entire familys faith was sure Mattie would wake up.

Leona walked over to the sink and started scrubbing the breakfast dishes, humming and moaning just a little louder than normal. It was an unusual type of worship, not customary for such a God-fearing woman as Leona Fitch.

Out on the porch, the tone caught Dozier's ear causing the hairs to raise up on the back of his neck. He realized how strong of an enemy sadness was. And it had moved in and was trying to take over the hearts and minds of the entire Fitch clan. He had to be fervent and effectual because they depended on his strength.

"Leona," yelled Dozier. "Come on out a minute and looky dis here."

"What is it, Dozier?" Leona replied, drying her hands on the apron front. "I thought you'd gone out to da field."

To Leona's surprise, the entire family had gathered in front of the house staring up into the sky in amazement.

"This here is the same kinda strange color that was in the sky when Mattie fell in da creek," said Michael solemnly.

This caused the others to mumble in agreement.

"Whatcha think it means, pa?"

"You reckon it's a sign?" asked Jay innocently.

"Never can tell, son, but it don't hurt to believe that sumthin's 'bout to change."

"Oh yes, sumthin's bout to change, I can feel it deep down, it's like a fire shut up in my bones," cried Leona. "I been prayin' and this here is the sign."

Dozier nodded in agreement. "I been thinking that myself. We just gon' wait and see how this here day goes."

The boys shrugged, mumbled amongst themselves and headed out toward the field.

Dozier and Leona began admiring the sunflowers, which always stood as a perfect reminder of Mattie. Off in the distance they could see Pamela and Pauline walking towards them as they had done every morning since the accident.

"Hey!" cried Pamela, who began running towards them full speed. "Do y'all see the sky?"

"Yes indeed Miss Pamela, we been lookin' at it all mornin' long," said Dozier and Leona in unison.

This was followed by a brief pause while Pauline caught up and joined the rest of them, staring inquisitively at the colored sky. The close examination was followed by a string of questions intermingled with scratched heads, cleared throats and an overall feeling of uneasiness.

The only one who actually seemed in control was Pamela. She had dreamed about Mattie the night before and was sure that this occurrence was a sign.

"I'm gonna go on in and see Mattie if it's all right," said Pamela. Then she pulled up the bottom of her dress and headed up the steps. "This is a great day!"

"Pamela," cried Leona, which caused everyone to stop cold.

Leona hesitated.

"Yes ma'am," Pamela replied, never looking back.

"You're a good friend," she said calmly.

No one spoke for a moment. Suddenly a brisk wind blew across the porch sending the faint aroma of lavender from the adjacent field. The sunflowers began swaying back and forth rhythmically.

"Yes, she is," said Pamela at last. "And today is a good day for miracles to happen."

Pauline swallowed, but said nothing.

After a few minutes Leona and Pauline walked into the house to check on the girls, while Dozier headed out to the field once again feeling pain in his gut about Mattie's sleep and trying to make sense of the color in the sky.

Back inside the house Pamela, Pauline and Leona were busy tending to Mattie as she slept. Leona, combing Mattie's hair, began to sing in a whisper, "this little light of mine, I'm gonna let it shine," Mattie's favorite song. The others joined in the serenade.

About an hour or so later Pamela sat gently on the bed next to Mattie and grabbed her hand. Leaning in she whispered, "Hey Mattie, remember our pinkie promise? Well you gotta wake up so we can—Oh my!" she gasped, "Look!"

All at once beads of sweat began to form on Mattie's brow. Her tiny hands became cold and clammy. Pauline headed quickly over to the bureau and dipped a cloth in cool water and placed it gently on her forehead.

"Mattie, Mattie,' Leona whispered, "It's me, Mama, can you hear me child?"

Leona closed her eyes, squeezing Mattie cool moist hands, and began to pray. Pamela moved to the opposite side of the bed, knelt down and began to shout into the crumpled blanket.

"MATTIE! MATTIE!!" she yelled emotionally. "Please wake up!"

She lifted her face to see if her outbursts were having any affect on Mattie, and she smiled. "Mattie would just tell me to hush all that yellin', but I figured it may help."

"Mattie's gon' wake up when her time is right, Miss Pamela, and not 'til then I reckon," said Leona solemnly.

"We won't give up though. Never," said Pauline, still wiping the drops of moisture from Mattie's forehead. "She is just asleep and when she's ready to wake up then that's what's gonna happen."

"I'm reckon I'm ready then," said Mattie, in a weak raspy voice.

The room went silent. No one spoke.

"My Lord, child, oh my Lord!" said Leona frantically. "Run and get the Doc, Miss Pamela." Leona grabbed Mattie and began kissing her forehead while she reached lovingly around her frail body lifting her upright.

Pamela stood in shock. She was frozen.

"Pamela, wake up child, hurry!" yelled Pauline, "I'll go for Dozier."

The front screen flew open as Pamela burst through it, then out and down the steps. Looking over toward the field she yelled hysterically at Dozier and the boys, "Mattie's woke, hurry!"

Dozier stood up slowly, and glanced toward Pamela who was quickly approaching the end of the road, then back to the house, his heart pounding. *Did she just say*

Mattie was woke, he thought? Time seemed to stand still and proceeded gradually into slow motion. He could hear his garbled voice yelling to his sons, but nothing made sense.

Pauline was standing at the edge of the field yelling at the top of her lungs.

"Pa, let's go, Mattie's woke!" The boys spoke in unison. They ran to and grabbed Dozier who still had not moved, "Come on Pa!"

They entered the house and hurried down the hall to Mattie's room. The whole house was quickly filled with overwhelming excitement and joyous energy. The news spread quickly around the town, that little Mattie had awakened from her sleep. Before long many of those who knew and loved Mattie, old and young, were standing around outside hoping to get a chance to see her.

The family gathered around her bed. Smiles and laughter were escaping through every pore that had been closed since the shutting of her eyes. Doc and Pamela pressed their way through the crowd, into the house and into Mattie's room.

"Hi Doc Austin, how are you today," she said between sips of water.

"Not too much now Mattie, save your strength," said Leona cautiously.

"I'm fine mama, you'll see," she replied.

"Well now, Miss Mattie, I'll be the judge of that," said Doc, firmly. "Now if I can have y'all step outside for just a bit, I want to check this little angel out for a minute and see if she doing as well as she lookin'."

"Papa, Mama, I want Pamela to stay, too, if'n that's all right, Doc Austin, sir," said Mattie, respectfully.

"Well, I reckon that will be just fine."

Hesitantly, the others left the room, immediately pressing their ears against the thin wood planks, listening intently.

About twenty minutes later Doc Austin emerged from the room grinning from ear to ear, and shaking his head in disbelief.

"That's an amazing child, I must say."

"Whatcha mean, Doc?"

"Go on in and see for yourself."

Doc came through the front door and swaggered down the front steps, holding tightly to his worn black bag, his polished wood pipe resting safely between his teeth.

"All is well, folks," said Doc with confidence. He stopped and placed the bag on the ground, striking a match and lighting his pipe. "She is resting nicely and it looks like she's gon' be just fine," puffing lightly on his pipe, "so go on home and let her rest, but all is well."

Back inside Mattie had begun to tell her family about the journeys that she had taken part in while she was asleep. Everyone was huddled around the bed staring in amazement, fixed on every word.

Mattie's eyes were shining brightly as she laughed openly at the fuss everyone seemed to make about an event that she could not remember.

"I met this young fella name Deuce, and another one named Chris, and then a girl, Veronica, and I looked different each time except with Chris," said Mattie, sitting up against the pillows. "I was an old lady, then I was a dancer, too, Mama, but I was right there with them, I was like an angel."

The room went silent. Mattie looked around and thought, what did I say wrong?

"That sounds like so much fun, Mattie, tell me more!" cried Pamela

"No, no, Pamela, Mattie needs to rest, it has been a full morning already," said Pauline nervously.

"I fine, Miss Pauline," squeaked Mattie.

"I think you need to rest, Mattie," said Dozier sternly. "You can tell your dreams later."

Mattie took a deep breath.

"I saved their lives, and I want to tell you at least one, please, Papa."

"All right, Mattie," said Dozier, looking over at Leona for support. "Just one."

Everyone took a seat and listened attentively.

"I was an old lady this time, and this young boy named Deuce who had given up on his dreams because of all the bad stuff that had happened to his family…."

No one moved.

The Graduates

Four years passed so quickly, and seeing Mattie again was the only thing that Deuce could think about once the excitement wore off with the family. He had to show her the acceptance letter to law school, thank her for believing in him and showing him that there was more than one road to choose. He got his things together and headed down to the square to meet her.

Arriving a few minutes early he took a seat on a bench by the pier and waited patiently for Mattie to arrive.

It had been a tough four years for Chris, but thanks to Mattie being true to himself was first and foremost, and accepting help was no longer a concern. The draft came and he was going to the NBA, his dream-come-true. A few words from the mouth of a child changed his life forever. Chris got up early, and spent the morning preparing for seeing Mattie, the little girl who helped him see through to himself. He gathered his things, and headed down to the square; arriving about five minutes early he leaned against the rail of the pier and waited.

The celebration was like no other. The restaurant was filled inside and out with balloons and beautifully decorated banners and a large piñata. It had been a long four years for the Luna family. Not so long for Veronica who had traveled the globe dancing with the theatre, and now after many long years had landed a principal role on Broadway. The studio was filled with the sounds of children yelling and laughing as they participated in self-defense lessons. Veronica, looking through the window, smiled as the memories of dancing with Mattie flashed back.

Veronica woke up early and stared blankly at the ceiling. Today she would see Mattie and they would dance again. She gathered her things and headed toward the square. Excitement filled the car, and the advertisement of the Broadway show lay still in her lap. Arriving a few minutes early she headed toward the pier and looked for a place to wait.

About thirty minutes passed and there was no sign of Mattie, and Deuce, Chris and Veronica, separately but collectively were becoming nervous.

Mattie was always punctual and spoke of the importance of being on time, they thought, separately.

Chris looked over at the bench, nodded hello at DJ who responded, and looked suspiciously at Veronica who was leaning against the railing.

Each one started to stare at the other, wondering why each of them was there and did not really seem to be doing anything. The breeze of the bay and the yachts parked along the waterway had held their attention for some time but now things were becoming strange.

"Excuse me, I was meeting a friend here and I was wondering if you saw anyone else standing around? It's not like her to be late," said Veronica, curiously.

"No, I haven't seen anyone. I'm waiting on someone myself, and I'm starting to get a little worried because she is older," replied Deuce.

"Me, too," said Chris.

Meeting at the bench the three sat down together. Not sure of what to say next they continued to wait, playing with their cell phones to pass the time.

"My name is Veronica."

"I'm Deuce," he said, looking over at Chris.

"Oh, what's up, I'm Chris."

"You play ball, right?" said Deuce.

"Yeah, I just graduated and got picked up."

"Yeah, I know; I watched the draft. Congratulations," said Deuce, interrupting. "I thought you looked familiar."

Suddenly Veronica, tired of the sports talk, spoke up. "Mattie, where are you?"

Both Chris and Deuce turned quickly.

"Who did you say?" he asked, stunned.

"Mattie, she is my dance teacher, and I am supposed to meet her here at noon," said Veronica.

"Dance teacher?" Chris responded sharply. "She is only twelve. How can she be a dance teacher?"

"Twelve? Mattie is about eighty years old," said Deuce, clearly confused.

"Come on now, what is going on here?" said Chris in a puzzled tone. "Maybe we just know three different Mattie's, and they told each of us to meet here at noon. Man, I don't know, this is a trip."

Deuce stood up and didn't say anything. He took a deep breath, turned around and stared at Chris and Veronica.

"Is the Mattie you know from South Carolina?"

There was silence. Their hearts were pounding and heads spinning.

Veronica stared at the ground trying to pretend that she didn't hear the question, but there was no arguing with this. Her eyes filled with tears.

"Yeah," clearing her throat, "the Mattie I know is from Darlington, South Carolina, to be exact."

"Oh man," yelled Chris, "you gotta be kiddin'! Man, this is a trip. How can we all know a Mattie and she be three different people, three different ages, but be from the same place? Come on man, what is this?"

"Okay, wait a minute. Let's try to figure this out," said Deuce, tapping his finger on the side of his head. "I met her about four years ago. What about you?"

"Me too," said Chris.

"Yeah, I did too."

Again, there was silence, broken by the sound of a honking horn circling the roundabout. Veronica, fearing another addition to an already scary situation, looked back and forth waiting for someone to say anything that would make sense. A couple of minutes passed.

"Do you think that—ummmm, never mind," she said nervously.

"What? Say it, because I think we are all thinking the same thing even though we aren't saying it," said Deuce, looking perplexed.

"Man I don't know about you, but that would be crazy if she is the same person. Man, I'm tellin' you, my mind can't even get around that, for real," said Chris.

"I thought I was the only one thinkin' that, said Deuce.

"Me too," said Veronica, giggling. "This is crazy."

For the next few hours they sat on that bench comparing lives, exchanging information and sharing stories of their time with Mattie, and how she impacted their lives.

Night rolled in bringing a cool breeze off the bay, laughter and people onto the square. Time had passed so quickly.

"We are going to have to find out where she is, or what happened to her. I have to know something," said Veronica.

"Back at school one of my criminal justice professors has some connections and I'm thinking that I can give him a call and see if he can help us out," said DJ excitedly.

"Aw man, that sounds cool. Do you think he will be able to?" said Chris.

"I have complete confidence in this man; he is as tough as nails, and smarter than most. If anyone can help us it's him."

Veronica raised an eyebrow.

"What if he thinks we're crazy?" Veronica responded quickly, tapping her nails on the side of the bench. "This sounds crazy to us. What if he doesn't believe us? What if no one believes us?"

"Don't even trip, we know lots of people in high places now that we are on the right track, and all we have to do is tell them that we all knew this girl who was twelve when I met her, and when you met her she was 30, and……… man….they are gonna thing we're crazy."

"I have an idea," said Deuce, grinning at the two of them.

"Well, what's up?" said Chris. "We gotta do something."

"I will ask my professor as if it's for someone else, you know, get his opinion about how to find someone, and then we'll do the rest ourselves, and then no one has to know," said Deuce eagerly.

He took out his PDA and began text messaging frantically. "I hope he gets right back to me."

This seemed to take Veronica and Chris's mind off of the drama for a moment; it was their only hope at this point. They headed down the ramp admiring all of the boats and yachts parked alongside. A man, dressed in boating attire, was rinsing off the deck of his boat, smiling at them as they passed

"So you're going to the NBA?" said Veronica, trying to make small talk.

"Yeah, I owe my getting into college to Mattie. She really helped me out," said Chris.

"It sounds like she helped us all out. Do you believe in angels?" Veronica asked suspiciously.

"You know, I'm not sure of what to think anymore. This is strange and who knows what will happen when it's all over with, you know? All I know is she can't possibly be three different people at the same place at the same time without there being some kind of spiritual stuff happening. It's sort of spooky."

"Hey!" yelled Deuce. "He's calling, come on!"

Chris and Veronica turned and caught a glimpse of Deuce waving frantically from the top of the boat ramp in a split second they headed back up the ramp and over the walkway. He was listening intently on the phone.

Deuce turned around to look at Veronica and Chris who appeared both nervous and excited.

"Well thank you sir. I appreciate your help and," pausing for a moment,"yes sir, I will, thank you, goodbye."

"What happened?" Chris asked Deuce excitedly.

"Well, he's pretty smart, and asked me a whole lot of cop-type questions, but that's what happens when you talk to someone who used to work for the FBI."

"FBI, what?" said Chris, "You gotta be kidding, dog. Your professor use to work for them, he's gonna know something's up man. They don't miss anything."

"That's true, but we haven't done anything wrong; we're just asking questions to try and find somebody who doesn't seem to exist." "If anything he'll think we're crazy," said Veronica, overwhelmed.

"Calm down, it's all right, but we need to get a game plan so that we can figure out what is going on. It's too late to do anything now so let's hook up tomorrow and get started," Deuce said, reaching back in his pocket for the PDA. "Okay, let's exchange numbers and is eleven o'clock good for you?" pointing to Veronica and Chris.

"Yeah, that's fine," they replied in unison.

"Okay, when you get home if you have a computer get on it, and see if you can connect anything with what

Mattie had talked to you about—you know, her family, friends, anything. We got a lot of work to do."

Slowly, the three new friends headed towards the parking lot, each in their own silence.

Their meetings over the course of the next couple of weeks proved futile, running into dead ends at every turn. Frustration replaced excitement. The sound of Mattie's voice played over and over in their minds, but the feelings of madness and confusion waited in the wings. The three had begun to give up any chance of finding Mattie, or making sense of her connection to them.

Then a break came.

It was a beautiful cloudless early summer day. There was a warm breeze and the streets were filled with people who seemed to be aware of something special in the air. Deuce sent a text message asking them to meet him at the library; he had some exciting news.

Veronica and Chris arrived at the same time and entered quietly and began looking around for Deuce.

The librarian stood staunchly behind the counter with an old grey suit, silver hair rolled tightly in a bun, barely smiling, and hushing a few people talking into lower voices. There were rows and rows of bookcases, filled with worn unused books, and the smell of old was in the air. It felt lonely. Veronica and Chris looked up and down each aisle until falling upon Deuce hidden in a back corner looking intently at the computer screen.

"Hey, there you are. We been looking all over for you," said Veronica in a whisper.

"Man, tell me you have some good news," said Chris, with an anxious look.

"I got a call from my professor this morning, and he found something," said Deuce, calmly. There was complete silence.

"Say something, don't make us wait. What's up?" said Veronica, in a loud voice.

"Yeah man, come on, don't play around," Chris responded.

The sound of hush came from the librarian responding to the excitement in the rear.

"Shh, okay, okay. We found where she lives in South Carolina," said Deuce, earnestly, "but there's one more thing."

"What is it now? Please don't tell me nothing crazy because I don't think I could take another surprise," said Chris suddenly.

"Me either, I just want to know what's going on, I just want to see Mattie again and tell her thanks. That's all I wanted to do," said Veronica nervously as Deuce handed them envelopes with their names on them. "What's this?" they asked in unison.

"Tickets," Deuce responded nonchalantly.

"Tickets? For what?" said Chris, tone sounding confused?

"Huh, what's going on?" asked Veronica.

"We're goin' to South Carolina," said Deuce, frankly. "He's really got something, he wouldn't go into detail but he has everything set up for us, tickets, everything. All we have to do is get to the airport."

"You gotta be kidding, oh my God," said Veronica suddenly. "We are going to South Carolina! He found Mattie? Wow, what's goin' on?"

Chris raised an eyebrow. "Man, don't play with my head, I can't take it dawg, for real?"

"I don't know either but we are getting to go where Mattie's from, and find out what is really goin' on."

Suddenly a warm breeze entered through an open window bringing with it a familiar scent causing flashbacks to occur collectively. The sounds of Mattie's voice began to play over and over in their minds, and calm filled the room.

There was a moment of peaceful silence. Suddenly Deuce laughed openly causing Veronica and Chris to join in, as he began to gather up his papers off of the table.

"Well, are you in?" asked Deuce.

Veronica took a deep breath, trying to enjoy the last moments of the vanishing fragrance. She looked both nervously and reluctantly at Deuce who was waiting patiently.

"I'm in," she said.

"You know I'm in, when do we leave?" said Chris.

Deuce got to his feet and picked up the rest of his things, looked over, very subdued, at Veronica who looked as if she was going to burst, and quietly responded, "Friday."

The week seemed to creep at a snail's pace, and the anticipation was more than they could bare, but finally Friday arrived and they would finally find Mattie.

The airport was busy with summer travelers, the sound of honking horns, crying babies, and impatient officers standing curbside shooing weary waiters away from the curb. The smell of jet fuel, men's cologne and women's perfume caused the atmosphere to fill with a buzz, bringing alive all of their senses. After a few curious and excited looks the car stopped and they exited one by one.

Deuce, Veronica and Chris eagerly approached the ticket counter. They were greeted by a lovely young woman, in a perfectly ironed uniform, with piercing hazel eyes, and hair that seemed to massage her shoulders and a striking smile. "Hi, how are you?" Deuce said in a flirting tone.

"I'm well, thank you, and may I have your tickets, please?" she said.

"Let's go fellas," said Veronica, giggling. "A woman's work is never done."

"Whatever, girl," said Chris awkwardly. "I was just getting ready to put the real game on her, and we would have had those seats anyway."

"That's what the problem is, Chris; women don't want game, we want integrity, at least most of us."

"Aww, I didn't mean like that, but I know eventually I would have gotten the seats."

"Yeah but the plane leaves today dawg, we don't have that much time," said Deuce, laughing, causing the others to join in.

"There you go, whatever dude. It's cool," he said, chuckling.

It had been a pleasant beginning to what would be a comfortable flight.

Deuce, Chris and Veronica eagerly exited that plane and followed the rest of the passengers, but bypassed baggage claim. Their trip wasn't quite over since they had to mentally prepare themselves to take making the two-hour drive from Columbia into Darlington.

The professor had set up a driver to take them on the next leg of the journey, so as the doors slid open they got a taste of the South Carolina summer weather up close and personal. The muggy heat entered their nostrils and sent sweat immediately pouring out of every gland and pore in their bodies. A slight breeze offered no relief from the high temperature as their comfortable California clothes quickly became sticky, clammy southern garments.

"Oh my goodness, it is hot out here," gasped Veronica.

"You are right about that, I'm already starting to sweat, let's find that dude and get out of this heat," said Deuce, pointing to a man at the end holding a sign that read.

"Where, man? This is crazy," said Chris with a pleading look.

"Right there," he replied.

Veronica and Chris turned and noticed, from a distance, a tall, slender, elderly man holding a sign with their names printed boldly across the front. They waved in relief.

As they approached the gentleman he was standing, it seemed, in front of a beat-up, old jalopy that had seen better days. He smiled kindly, giving way to his unbelievably white teeth and perfectly manicured moustache which sat comfortably atop his thin lips. His grey Afro was round like the moon, puffed proudly from underneath his cap that leaned ever so slightly to the side. He wore a tight black suit that looked a size or two too small, the pants slightly elevated, showing thick white socks that clashed with his black penny loafer shoes. He didn't seem to even break a sweat.

Although his clothes didn't fit his body, his calm exterior gave way to a peaceful disposition.

"Hi, I'm Deuce, this is Veronica and Chris," said Deuce, putting his bag on the ground.

"It is a pleasure to meet you. My name is Mel and I'm gonna be driving you down to Darlington. You folks have a good flight?" he asked, politely, picking up the bag and walking around the jalopy to the trunk of a beautiful black Mercedes.

"This is what we're ridin' in?" said Chris, rubbing his hands together.

"Why, yes sir is it sufficient."

"Oh yes, this is just fine. It's really beautiful," said Veronica, happily.

They all got into the car and seemed to study their surroundings silently for a few minutes. Then Mel said, "Just make you comfortable. We got a long ride, but we'll be there before you know it."

They nestled back into the black leather seats while the air conditioner blew cool air against their hot faces, and the sun, now sitting high, tried unsuccessfully to beam through the blacked-out windows.

The ride was comfortable and the scenery relaxing. The excitement of finally finding out the mystery of Mattie Fitch welled up in each one as they dozed in and out of consciousness.

Deuce laid back, his head pressed firmly against the backseat, not saying a word. Looking out of the car window at the landscapes of green and yellow, he reflected on Mattie, and what they would find. Resigned to the fact that the news would not be good, he placed his head in his hands and silently prayed himself to sleep.

"Are we almost there?" whispered Chris, leaning forward.

"Yes indeed, we should be there in about ten minutes, I reckon," said Mel, looking into the rear view mirror and smiling gently.

Chris slid back, looking over at Veronica and Deuce who were still sleeping. Suddenly he had a cold, damp feeling and small beads of sweat began to form on his brow. He started to think about Mattie, and what was waiting for them in Darlington.

Then, suddenly, as if they knew Darlington was approaching; calm lulled Veronica and Deuce out of their sleep.

"It's about time you guys woke up," said Chris fidgeting. "We're almost there, and I've been sitting here tripping off this whole thing. Man, it's got me a little nervous."

"I had the weirdest dream about Mattie, too," said Veronica, anxiously.

"I think Chris is right; the entire situation is a little strange but at the same time it's cool, you know. I don't have a scared feeling, it's more confusing," said Deuce, staring straight ahead.

After what seemed like forever, a sign appeared; **Darlington 5 miles.**

"I hope you all find what you looking for here, but it sounds to me like you've found it already," said Mel in a soft voice.

"Well, if you want to know the truth, we each saw, or uh…knew Mattie differently, said Deuce, hesitantly.

"Whatcha mean by that?" asked Mel, strangely.

There was complete silence.

Suddenly the back window lowered, sending a warm breeze in and around the car, startling all of them. Mel was watching them suspiciously in the rearview mirror.

In an instant, the window was up and the excitement gone. Veronica squeezed both Deuce and Chris's hands tightly as they tried to gather their thoughts.

Chris started to talk but knew he didn't have a clear idea of how he could explain something so confusing, so he sat back, cleared his throat and looked expectantly over at Deuce and Veronica. They were watching as he attempted to explain. But all each of them knew was that no one in their right mind would ever believe such a story.

"Were you gonna say something?" asked Mel.

"Umm…you know….I ……knew…uh…okay, first of all this is not going to make a lot of sense and you may think we are crazy but I met Mattie when she was old," said Deuce, shaking his head, brows raised.

"Yeah, and I knew her when she was around thirty, said Veronica, looking at Chris.

"She was about twelve when I met her."

Mel went completely quiet for a moment, staring at them. The car came to an abrupt stop; he looked both ways, coughed loudly and sped down the road. Deuce, Veronica and Chris watched him both anxiously and nervously, clutching the headrests.

"Is everything all right?" asked Deuce. "Are you okay?"

Mel fell silent. Out of sight of the children, his eyes filled with tears.

"Did we say something wrong?" said Veronica cautiously, leaning forward, lightly touching his shoulder.

Mel shook his head, but never spoke again.

Veronica glanced over at Deuce and Chris who shook their heads and motioned for her to sit back.

"Just leave him alone," whispered Chris, his finger to his lips. "Something weird is going on."

In agreement, they sat back quietly.

In the distance they could see Mattie's hometown was fast approaching. There were now almost seven thousand people, unlike what she had described as a child growing up, except the love of family, the hospitality and history of the people who made Darlington their home. This small country town had gone from dusty roads to a proudly fostered public square, a corner store, one filling station, and a famous speedway; to paved roads, spacious brick homes with screened in porches and green grass that grew freely, without boundaries. Sadly, it still showcased the railroad track that separated two sides of town, and people from one another.

Now they were heading into that same place. They sat up straight, filled with excitement, determined not to blink with a fear they would miss something. Mel drove slowly to allow them to take in the history and scenery of a town that seemed to have been created from legends. Through their sparkling eyes it was even more beautiful than Mattie had said; the little rural town she had spoken of with such admiration had seen a makeover. There were a few old dilapidated shacks that stood alone in the distance on acres of land where they had once been the haven for a poor sharecropper and his family.

"How far are we from the Miles residence?" said Deuce eagerly.

"It's just right up the road a piece. I reckon we should be there in about five minutes or so," said Mel softly. "I'm happy you folks will finally find what you have been looking for."

"Do you think we'll find something there?" said Chris.

"Where?" asked Mel.

"At the Miles place," he responded, leaning in.

"I guess it depends on why you're looking." He paused. "I remember the old folks use to say be careful what you look for, 'cause you may find it."

Chris moved closer to Mel, and looked over the seat to observe a tear-stained handkerchief sitting in his lap.

"You are looking for anything, Mel?"

"I was, but I found it today, thanks to you and your friends."

"Huh?" said Chris, in a confused tone. "How did we help you find something?"

"I reckon one of these days we'll all understand the reason why things happen like they do, but in the meantime we just keep right on living and trying to be the best we can, with what we got."

"Personally, I never believed in anything until I met Mattie," said Veronica, confidently. "But I notice with her it was more like helping me to figure it out myself without telling me what to do---which made it a whole lot easier than when your parents try to get you understand, you know."

"I know what you mean. My grandmother died and she was my every thing next to my Mom. But my Mom was busy with school and recovery, and the streets are ready for you when you have a lot of time on your hands," said Deuce. "But Mattie, she came right on time, just when I needed her. I couldn't have asked for more than that."

"It sounds like Mattie did a lot of life-changing for you all and I guess it don't matter how she came, but that she did."

They continued chatting as Mel drove slowly through town.

"Look over there," said Veronica, pointing toward a very large tree. "I think that's the Giant that Mattie talked about, where she would swing."

"I think you're right," yelled Deuce and Chris in agreement.

"Oh yes, that's the Giant, and the old creek," said Mel suspiciously.

"Can you pull over?"

"We don't have time; you supposed to be over to this residence right at noon because Miss has a schedule to keep," he said nervously.

"Well, can you take us later?"

"I reckon I can, we'll have plenty of time later."

Not long after they turned down a long, black-paved, tree and flower-lined driveway, the ride as smooth as silk. The grounds were tranquil and peaceful. In the distance stood a magnificent plantation home, with white columns that stood erect like four guards protecting the inhabitants. Off to the left, adjacent to the white home, situated in what appeared to be wild flowers and tall grass was a wooden two-story house, old and mysterious.

None of them spoke as they approached the house. Each one was wondering what the other was thinking, but never mumbled a word.

As they drew near the front of the house they noticed a tall slender woman posted caringly behind an old woman in a wheelchair, covered carefully with beautifully colored quilts.

The car came to a stop. No one moved.

A moment later, Mel turned around and faced them as they sat motionless in the backseat, looking pale.

"Well here we are, you gonna get out?"

Deuce sighed deeply.

Relieved, Veronica unbuckled her seatbelt and scooted forward. "I thought I was dreaming, and then I heard you breathe–"

"No I'm alive and well, just trippin', that's all. You think it's Mattie?" Deuce replied, uncomfortably.

"Man," said Chris, in an uneasy tone, "I'm feelin' real nervous."

"We came to find out, so come on," said Veronica.

"Yep, let's do this."

Exiting the car the three headed towards the steps where the old woman sat motionless in the wheelchair, her head down. Directly behind her stood a very serious-looking woman, wearing a perfectly ironed white dress, pale-colored stockings and black, buckled shoes. The nurse's cap sat perfectly atop her tightly pinned bun.

They stood frozen, unable to look away from her beautiful eyes, which for some strange reason looked very familiar.

Approaching cautiously, and smiling nervously, they were greeted with a simple nod from the nurse. Tapping the old woman lightly she leaned over and whispered.

"The children are here, Miss Pamela."

Suddenly, they were drawn in. She was old and frail, but captured an essence of time in every wrinkle which made its way across her visibly tired face. Her hair was aged, a soft gray. Her body was as thin and delicate as the leaves blowing in a warm spring day.

They paused, drawn into the peace that reflected heaven in her eyes, which were blue as shimmering ice. As she glanced upward they had a brief reflection of heaven.

"Well hello there, I have been waiting a long time for this moment, and what a welcomed sight you are," she whispered, in an audibly weak voice.

It's very nice to meet you Miss Pamela. I'm Deuce, and this is Veronica and Chris."

They all walked up the white concrete stairs and onto the porch where Pamela, now sitting straight up, was waiting energetically.

"Come on over, and sit a spell," said Pamela, pointing to white chairs with overstuffed pillows printed in sunflowers.

They each grabbed a chair and pulled closely around Pamela's chair, while Mel and the nurse began mumbling to one another by the car.

"What can I do for you?" Pamela muttered.

It took a few seconds for them to get their words together. Then Chris scooted closer and said what everyone else wanted to.

"We are trying to find Mattie Fitch, and apparently you must know her otherwise we wouldn't be here," said Chris softly.

"We all met her about four years ago, and we were going to meet her and she never showed up, and it's—" said Deuce, interrupted by an outburst of laughter from Pamela.

"Lordy be, Mattie Fitch was right, the whole time I was the only one who really believed her. She said that one day you would come here, and I am so thankful that I lived long enough to see this day," said Pamela, giddily.

"What do you mean?" said Veronica, in a tone of shock. "How did she tell you we would be here? Where is she?"

"Okay this is crazy. What is going on, is Mattie here?" asked Deuce, excitedly.

"Well of course she is," smiled Pamela, animatedly. "You have made my dreams come true, and Mattie Fitch,

I have done what you asked me, now I can go on and be at peace."

Deuce, Veronica and Chris, now standing, listened with their mouths slightly gaped and eyes wide open. There was a strong sense of nervousness floating in the air, engulfing all of them. Pamela's words were conflicting with everything that they knew to be true and Mel and the nurse stood unaffected by the entire scenario. Feelings of anxiousness and worry came over each of them.

All of a sudden a sense of calm filled the porch as a warm breeze surrounded them with the scent of lavender.

"There she is. I knew she'd show up," said Pamela, pointing toward a patch of sunflowers. "Come on here, Laura-Ann, push me on down to where Mattie is."

Looking back, Pamela motioned for them to follow her, as the nurse began to roll the chair down a long ramp attached to the side of the porch which led down to the sunflowers.

"I know I sound a little bit strange, but once we see Mattie we'll go back to house and have a long talk."

They went reluctantly. Their hearts were beginning to beat rapidly as the neared the sunflowers. The wildflowers and leaves swayed lightly in the warm breeze.

In a quick moment they were standing in front of the patch of sunflowers that seemed to smile brightly up at them, while wildflowers danced back and forth with excitement.

"Mattie, are you in there?" yelled Deuce.

"Oh yes, she's in there. Go on, Mel, show them where Mattie is," said Pamela, smiling widely.

As Mel stepped forward a hush filled the air. Veronica grabbed the arm sleeve of Deuce's jacket. Chris, holding his breath, had taken a couple of steps back ignoring the other two.

Pushing back the flowers gently, Mel looked back and pointed inside. "Why here is Mattie."

Veronica and Deuce turned around and motioned for Chris. "Let's do this together," said Deuce strongly.

He grabbed Veronica with one hand, and lightly pulled Chris forward with the other. Deuce was just one step ahead of them as he entered in. He stopped cold.

"What's wrong, Deuce," whispered Veronica.

There was not a sound, only a light breeze of hot wind, and a faint smell of lavender.

"Man say something, dawg. What's up?" said Chris in a nervous tone.

"Get in here," urged Deuce. "You won't believe this."

For a moment they stood motionless. Nothing could have prepared them.

Deuce glanced over his shoulder, "Come on, you gotta see this."

"I can't wait another minute, let's go," said Chris, grabbing Veronica and stepping through.

Suddenly Pamela spoke, her voice weak and raspy.

"Mattie Fitch, this here is the kids you told us about. They have come to see you. You said they would come—you was telling the truth the whole time; I remember folks thought you had gone crazy after your accident but we always believed you, Mattie Fitch, we always did, and I miss you Mattie."

Suddenly a gush of cool wind carrying a strong fragrance of lavender whisked around them causing Pamela, Mel and the nurse to laugh.

Directly ahead a beautiful angel atop a simple grave stone which read:

Mattie L. Fitch
"The Living Angel"
Born: April 28, 1917
Died: Unknown

About one minute passed. With silence filling the flower patch.

"I never thought it would end like this," said Chris somberly, the others agreeing.

"End, child? This is just the beginning," said Pamela laughing.

Acknowledgements

This is a great opportunity for me to acknowledge those that have played an intricate role in getting The Dreams of Mattie Fitch to you, the reader. I thank:

Erica Glessing of Happy Publishing for believing in Mattie, and wanting to share our story.

Kaarin Alisa for her beautiful spirit, friendship and great work on the website.

Martin Griffin Sr. for bringing Mattie Fitch to life in the beautiful artwork.

Anne Hedges for the editing which gave us a clear voice.

Daniel "Fig" Figueroa for assisting with the IT needs of Mattie and me.

Glen G Grace, for giving me my first online interview on "A Touch of Grace" and being an awesome mentor. Can't wait for my next interview!

Janice Edwards for giving me the television interview that changed my life. And for your kindness, and guidance. I can't wait for my next interview!

Leonard Szymczak and Ann McIndoo, two wonderful authors and friends for getting me motivated to start writing, and believing I could get it done!!